# LiTTLE GREEN MEN

## AT THE
## MERCURY INN

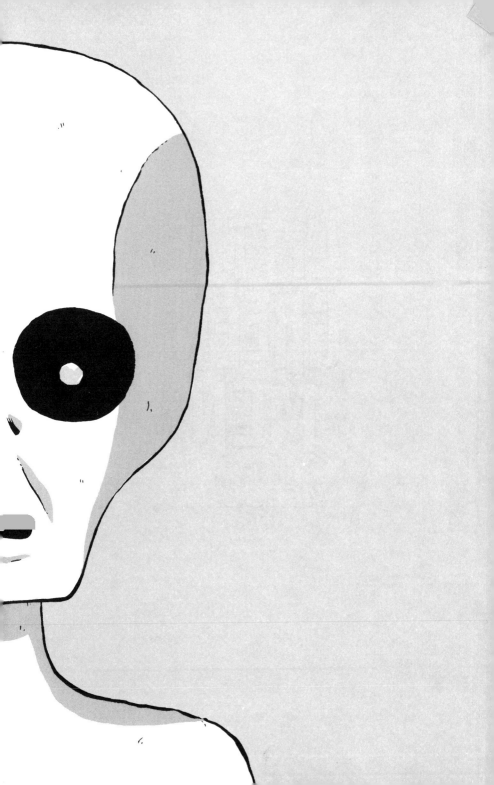

# LiTTLE GREEN MEN
## AT THE MERCURY INN

**GREG LEITICH SMITH**

**ILLUSTRATED BY**
**ANDREW ARNOLD**

ROARING BROOK PRESS
NEW YORK

Library of Congress Cataloging-in-Publication Data

Smith, Greg Leitich.
    Little green men at the Mercury Inn / Greg Leitich Smith ; illustrated
by Andrew Arnold. — First edition.
        pages cm
    Summary: "Two boys race to get an undercover alien back to her mothership
while dodging an oddball group of UFO-chasers, TV newspeople, and Florida
retirees"—Provided by publisher.
    ISBN 978-1-59643-835-4 (hardback)
    ISBN 978-1-62672-095-4 (ebook)
    [1.  Extraterrestrial beings—Fiction.   2.  Hotels, motels, etc.—Fiction.
3.  Florida—Fiction.   4.  Humorous stories.]   I.  Arnold, Andrew (Artist),
illustrator.   II.  Title.

PZ7.S6488Li 2014
[Fic]—dc23
                                                                    2013033527

Roaring Brook Press Books may be purchased for business or promotional use.
For information on bulk purchases please contact Macmillan Corporate and
Premium Sales Department at (800) 221-7945 x5442 or by email at
specialmarkets@macmillan.com.

First edition 2014
Book design by Andrew Arnold
Printed in the United States of America
by RR Donnelley & Sons Company, Harrisonburg, Virginia

1  3  5  7  9  10  8  6  4  2

FOR KEITH

# LITTLE GREEN MEN

## AT THE
## MERCURY INN

# 1

LIKE MOST OF HUMANITY THAT MORNING, I wasn't thinking at all about aliens from outer space.

I was thinking about garbage.

To be exact, I was confronting the piles of trash that the Williamses had left scattered around the courtyard and pool areas of the Mercury Inn and Suites the night before.

My parents owned the motel, and because any bit of food left out overnight attracted roaches the size of Volkswagens, sanitation was my life. That morning, my life was not so good.

Plastic wineglasses from the Williamses' anniversary party were strewn across the grass next to the koi pond. Paper plates and napkins lay beside the azaleas and underneath the coconut palms. Near the cocktail tables, a seagull pecked at an overflowing garbage can, knocking the remains of serving trays and chocolate layer cake to the ground beside it.

Staring at the job in front of me, I didn't really pay any attention to the telltale flip-flop of slippers behind me. I jumped when I felt a finger tap my shoulder.

"Did you hear what I said?"

It was Mrs. Fleance. She was decked out in what she called her "fancy" swim garb: a pink robe over a flowered swimsuit, fuzzy slippers that made slapping noises when she walked, and a swim cap with white plastic daisies. A blue-and-yellow beach towel and mirrored goggles were clutched in one hand, and a pair of flippers dangled from the other.

"Sorry," I said, shaking my head. "I must've spaced out."

Mrs. Fleance's eyes narrowed in that creepy way she had, and she pointed with the goggles. "Are you aware that there are a table and chairs at the bottom of the pool?"

"Yes, ma'am." I grabbed a garbage bag and shook it open. "But it's the deep end. They shouldn't really be in your way—"

"You know," Mrs. Fleance interrupted, "they don't have problems like this at the Ritz-Carlton." She crossed her arms and tapped her foot. Once.

"No, ma'am," I said again, and heroically didn't point out that we charged a lot less for an ocean view than the Ritz-Carlton. Also, they had a virtual army of all-night staff, and we had only José at the front desk and, occasionally, his grandsons, Jaime and Eduardo.

"Well?" Mrs. Fleance prompted.

I sighed. "I'll get them." I stepped around her and strode across the wooden bridge over the koi pond, past the new building, to the pool.

The "new building" wasn't really any newer than half the buildings at the motel, constructed when my parents did the big renovation just after I was born.

The Mercury Inn included an original lobby building with a diner off to the side and four two-story guest room buildings flanking the courtyard and koi pond (where the swimming pool used to be). The new building, with its ocean-view guest rooms and suites, sat opposite the lobby to enclose the courtyard on its fourth side. There was also a new pool, cabanas, and four cottages that each held two suites with their own ocean views.

When I reached the pool, Mrs. Fleance was right behind me. She took a step back as I pulled off my white Mercury Inn polo and tossed it onto a chaise. Then I kicked off my flip-flops, took a breath, and dived in.

The water felt cool and comfortable, a nice break from the morning humidity. I made a mental note to check the chlorine level later, after Mrs. Fleance had her swim and before I had to help get things ready for tonight's launch-viewing party.

I grabbed a chair and kicked my way to the surface, figuring I'd slide it up onto the deck and pick it up later. To my surprise, Mrs. Fleance took it from me and made a shooing motion. I dived back down, and we did the same with the rest of the furniture.

When I finally climbed out of the water, Mrs. Fleance reached into the pocket of her robe and handed me a quarter. "For now, don't worry about skimming the leaves."

"Thank you," I said as I stood there dripping.

With that, she dropped her robe onto a chaise, put on her goggles and flippers, jumped into the deep end, and began her laps.

"No lifeguard on duty," I muttered. I pressed water out of my hair and headed back to the garden area to finish cleaning.

The Mercury had been in the family since the late 1950s, when my grandparents built it as a motor inn during the first heyday of the space program. My mom and dad converted it into a quirky-but-upscale boutique motel a few years after they took it over.

Today, the guests were a mix of tourists, locals who wanted a quiet weekend getaway, and the occasional long-term resident, like Mrs. Fleance. A couple years ago, she sold her house and moved into the Skylab Suite because she "didn't want to mess with a condo" and liked getting free satellite TV. This never really made much sense to me, but she paid her rent on time and didn't make a lot of noise. She was a lousy tipper, though.

The Inn had a choice location right on the beach, within an easy walk of the Cocoa Beach Pier, not far from the flag-ship AP Sporting Goods and Surf Shop Extraordinaire (a division of AesProCorp, Inc.: "Do it like you mean it!"). As one of the only non-high-rises left on the Space Coast, and with features like the landscaped lap pool, luau pit, and clas-sic '50s diner and ice-cream parlor, the place was something of an attraction in its own right.

But the motel's biggest draws were the shindigs my par-ents threw for the manned space launches. Sure, you could get a close-up view at Jetty Park and, yes, you could see the shuttles on the pad from one of the parks up in Titusville. But ten seconds after liftoff, you got just as good a view from the beach in front of the motel.

And the launch parties out on the pool deck of the Mer-cury Inn and Suites were legendary.

With all that, you'd think that living in a motel would be fun. And it used to be. I used to really love being here all the time. I mean, it was a great place to be a kid—with the pool, the beach, the best ice cream on the Space Coast—but for the past year or two, it just hadn't felt like home. Probably because I spent most days on call 24/7 along with my parents, waiting on other people and cleaning up after them.

By the time I finished changing the garbage bags and picking up the trash, the sun had climbed all the way above the horizon. Marcia, who had started working at the diner sometime during Project Apollo, waved as she headed up the stairs to deliver bento box breakfasts to the Gemini Suite.

As I pitched a goblet into the garbage bag I'd hung from the maintenance cart, I noticed, on the other side of the pond, a cute and intense-looking girl with long black hair. She was sitting cross-legged between a pair of palmettos, in front of a bamboo bench, next to where the stepping-stones began at the water's edge. Every now and then, she tossed something from a white paper bag into the pond. A group of koi had schooled together in front of her, splashing and lunging for whatever she was throwing in.

It was Dru Tanaka. She had arrived at the motel with her parents the day before. Her father apparently worked for one of the contractors at the Cape. I wasn't sure about the details (neither were my parents), but the family was here for an indefinite stay, being paid for by Mr. Tanaka's employer. We didn't usually delve into the personal lives of our guests, but (a) the company had paid six months in advance, which was a huge deal, and (b) my mother had discovered they had "a child my age." Which, of course, she'd had to tell me like she'd done every time that had happened since I was three, and I wished she would stop.

I crossed over the stones to pick up a couple of goblets that had floated with the current. As I reached the last of them, Dru stared at me.

"You," she said in a flat monotone, "are dripping."

"Um, yeah," I replied, feeling suddenly awkward.

She was silent while I picked up the cup. Then, in a seamless motion, she stood, brushed off her black camouflage cargo pants, and straightened her black SeaWorld T-shirt. She crumpled the paper bag and held it out to me. As I took it, she spoke again. "Have you been here long?"

Which was an odd thing to ask. "Um, yes," I said. "I guess. I mean, I got here now for the cups, but I've lived at the motel all my life. My name's Aidan, by the way."

And the lines were so smoothly delivered, I felt my face turn red.

Dru stared at me with unblinking eyes. "Good." She brushed past and walked back out along the boardwalk to exit the courtyard.

When I looked down, I noticed small piles of white shell fragments Dru had placed around her. Five of them, each about the size of an ant mound; they were stark white against the black soil. I considered smoothing them into the dirt, but then caught sight of a green gecko sitting next to one. The lizard glanced up, then turned and dashed away under the nearest of the palmettos.

"Huh," I said aloud to nobody.

# 2

ONCE I GOT EVERYTHING CLEANED UP (AND
passed my mother's white glove inspection), I headed over
to the diner for breakfast. Mrs. Pompeia Jones—a member
of Mrs. Fleance's pinochle gang and a resident of 1-701—
was sitting near the back, so I made sure to take the booth
closest to the cash register and the door. From there, next
to the wall with the signed photos of celebrities and astronauts, I had a view into the motel lobby.

Marcia dropped off a bowl of fresh tropical fruit and
took my order. As I waited for her to bring my breakfast,
Louis and his sister, Erica, pulled up in Erica's new Mustang. Louis jumped out almost before the car had stopped.
Erica yelled something at him and then sped away.

Louis and I had been friends ever since I elbowed him in
the chin during a water polo game in third-grade gym class.

He helped out here at the motel and was kind of a sci-fi and UFO nut.

I nodded hello, but before either of us could say anything further, Mrs. Jones stepped up to the cash register and handed Marcia her check.

"You're getting to be pretty nimble on that leg of yours," she told Louis.

His face grew still like it usually did when people brought up his prosthetic.

Let me explain: About two years earlier, just after she'd gotten her driver's license, Erica was driving us home from a water polo match up in Edgewater. Louis had shotgun, and I was asleep in the back seat.

As we were going past Canaveral National Seashore, an ancient Chevy pickup truck ran a red light and smashed into our car. The other driver was impaled on the truck's steering column and died instantly; Erica broke her collarbone; and Louis lost his right leg just above the knee. I was unharmed, except for a scar on my forehead shaped like a lightning bolt.

Kidding. At least about the scar.

Anyway, a guy up in Gainesville at the joint AesProCorp-UF-NASA Prosthetics Engineering Group saw the story in the paper, and almost immediately Louis was fitted with a prototype high-tech leg and "smart knee." It was pretty similar to the ones our military veterans were getting, except it was outfitted to send real-time telemetry up to the lab at the university—the engineers said they'd "wanted to do some up-to-the-second monitoring and modeling on adolescent biomechanics."

It took a few months of getting used to, but the prosthetic seemed to have worked mostly without a hitch: Louis could run and go up stairs and bike and walk without that weird rotate-from-the-hip thing that you had to do with older prosthetics. And it looked cool, too: sort of black and matte gray metal and carbon fiber, which was the signature of the

AesProCorp sports equipment and clothing company, the prime sponsor of the project.

It wasn't nearly as bad as it could've been, since we weren't all dead. Although, to be honest, none of us saw it that way at the time.

The weirdest thing about the crash was Louis's story that he had seen a UFO just before the pickup hit us: a sphere, he told everyone, glowing blue-green, with rings around it, like Saturn.

Erica said she hadn't seen a thing, and the doctors figured it must've just been shock or something from the accident, Louis's mind misremembering the flashing lights from the ambulance.

Once he finished all the physical therapy, Louis's biggest complaint—even more than the phantom pain—was that no one believed him about the UFO.

Well, that and having to deal with the occasional odd comment about the leg. Like now.

Before Louis could do something we'd all regret, like pelt Mrs. Jones with fresh citrus fruit, Marcia had rung up the bill and handed Mrs. Jones her change.

For a moment longer, Louis was silent. Then he grabbed an orange from the basket on the table and rolled it around a couple times to loosen the peel. After tossing it once in his hand, he held it up to the light.

"It's an orange," I remarked. "This is Florida. We grow them here."

He grabbed two more and began juggling them, because he knew I've never been able to. "I nearly got arrested this morning."

"Oh?"

He chuckled, almost breaking his rhythm. "I took the boat out . . . They've expanded the no-fly and no-boating areas for tonight's launch."

"So?" I said. The exclusion zones around the Cape were designed to both keep civilian boats and aircraft out of harm's way and prevent them from harming the launching spacecraft.

"They never have before," Louis replied, "at least not on this late notice." He caught the oranges, setting them back in their basket, and leaned forward. "I heard a rumor on the UFO Boards that they did it because of the sighting over Baikonur last month."

I sighed. Supposedly, last month there had been inexplicable lights in the sky and a violation of restricted airspace during the most recent Soyuz resupply mission to the International Space Station. "Or it could've been because of the extra media attention."

Tonight's launch wasn't just a space launch. It was the first flight of the new space clipper, *Resolution*. The first in a new class of spacecraft designed to take us back to the moon and then to Mars and beyond. Originally, the launch was supposed to have taken place from Vandenberg in California, but it had been moved to Canaveral for no clear reason (Louis, of course, insisted it was because of increased UFO activity on the West Coast).

"I'm telling you," Louis said, "something is going on at the Cape tonight, and we've got to find out what."

"We have to work the party," I said. "We can watch the launch from here." It was usually our job to help set things up and arrange chairs and give a hand to the food servers and whoever else needed help.

"It's not just the launch," Louis whispered, taking a look around to see if anyone was listening. (They weren't.) Solemnly, he pulled something from his pocket and set it on the table in front of me. It was one of those rubber wristband things people wore to help fight cancer, only instead of being yellow, it was silver-gray. "Wear this."

"Are you proposing?" I asked, which was when I noticed he was wearing one, too.

"Shut up," he answered. "It's got embedded titanium particles to prevent the aliens from picking up your mental aura."

"Seriously?" I said. "For when a tinfoil hat just won't do?"

I'd never seen him this far overboard before. Sure, he'd always kind of geeked out about aliens and UFO's, especially after the accident, but this time it seemed like he thought he had firsthand knowledge of something. To humor him, I grabbed the wristband and put it on. "Are we expecting an alien invasion tonight?"

"My sources tell me something big is going to happen—" he began, but then clammed up when my father stepped into the diner from the lobby.

"Aidan," Dad said, "can you guys go check on the Apollo Suite?"

"Isn't that where the Tanakas are?" I asked.

My dad nodded. "It's probably nothing, but the guy downstairs from them called in a noise complaint. Go see if you can get them to keep it down, if necessary." He shrugged. "I'd do it myself, but . . ."

" 'But the Tanakas paid six months in advance,' " I quoted, "and you don't want to offend—"

"Well, not too much," Dad answered. "This way, I can blame my idiot twelve-year-old son for any misunderstanding."

"Thirteen," I said.

"Not until next month," he replied, "which you won't see unless you get moving."

Louis bit back a laugh, but I got up and headed out the door.

"Hold on. I'm coming, too." He caught up with me outside by the vending machines.

"Okay," I said. "So what's the plan for the alien invasion?"

"Shh!" he replied, grabbing my arm, again glancing around for eavesdroppers. "We'll talk later."

"Fine." We crossed the courtyard and took the stairs of the new building two at a time like we usually did.

As we walked up to the door of the Apollo Suite, I could see that the drapes were still drawn, and when I knocked, the door swung open.

"Hello?" I said as Louis followed me in.

"Go away!" a voice called. It wasn't really hospitable, but honestly, that's the reaction you got a good bit of the time, which tended to be hard on housekeeping.

The suite was one of the nicer ones: a 1950s-style living room seating area faced a very twenty-first-century flat screen television as you entered. A small desk and chair sat by the window. Beyond that was a dining area with an open kitchen off to the side. Doors for bedrooms, bathrooms, and closets opened from the main room. Windows, now covered with drapes, opened onto a view of the ocean or courtyard. And the whole place was done up in pastel and tropical blues, greens, and purples.

"What did you *do*?" I exclaimed as soon as my eyes adjusted to the dark.

The television was in pieces. The video panel rested at an angle, face out on the couch. Its innards—circuit boards and wires—were scattered on the coffee table.

My parents were going to totally freak out. The Apollo had been one of the first rooms to get the new flat screen TV upgrade. And they cost a fortune, even with the volume discount.

I stepped forward to get a closer look, but paused when I heard a high-pitched whine behind me. Louis froze in his

tracks and stared down at his knee. The sound was coming from the motor, a noise sort of like what happens when you accidentally step on a cat's tail, only quieter. Louis flexed the joint, shaking his head. I'd never heard it do that before, either.

After a moment, it went away.

"What was that?" I ventured.

He shook his head again and sat on the couch next to the TV. He tested the knee joint once more, and it seemed okay, so I turned back to the table. "Is that a soldering iron?"

Dru Tanaka was sitting on the easy chair next to the couch, hunched over the coffee table with the soldering iron and holding on to a circuit board. "The TV was making a buzzing noise."

"So you took it *apart*?" I said, my voice rising. "That's a brand-new wide-screen, high-definition TV!"

"It was making a buzzing noise," Dru repeated in a soothing tone. "Don't worry, I'll have it fixed up right away. Like new." She paused. "Better than new, to be precise. It won't have that buzzing noise anymore."

"But—" I began.

"After that, if there's anything wrong, I'm sure my parents will be happy to replace it." She waved the soldering iron at Louis. "I'm Dru, by the way."

"Louis," he said. "That's Aidan." He looked around. "Where *are* your folks?"

Dru just looked at me. "The integrated circuit," she said, "was independently invented by Jack Kilby of Texas Instruments and Robert Noyce of Fairchild Semiconductor."

"I know," I told her, because who doesn't?

Then Louis stood, taking a small step, testing the leg again.

"If you like," Dru said to him, gesturing again with the soldering iron, "when I'm done with this, I can take a look at your prosthetic."

"That's okay," he replied, gritting his teeth in annoyance, although it wasn't the worst thing anyone had ever said to him.

"My parents are out fishing," she said, almost after I'd forgotten the question. "There's a launch party tonight, yes?"

"Yup," Louis replied when I didn't. "It usually starts a couple hours before liftoff."

"Good," she said, still in her monotone. "I may be there early."

"But . . ." I gestured at the TV.

"It shouldn't take long to put this back together," Dru tried to assure me.

"You know," Louis said, "we should probably just call the shop and—"

"We don't have time to bother them with this," Dru interrupted. "Besides, I've probably voided the warranty."

Then she stood, took both Louis and me by our arms, and gently but firmly showed us outside. "Like I said, if there is a problem, my parents will replace it." She lowered her voice. "However, for the moment, I don't think there's any reason to tell anyone, do you?" She reached out to shake my hand and expertly held out a folded-up bill.

I, also expertly, took it. I kept my face expressionless as she closed the door in our faces.

Louis grabbed my arm to see what Dru had handed me.

"Downstairs. Now," I whispered as he was about to speak. When we entered the stairwell around the corner from the Apollo Suite, I unfolded the bill. "Fifty bucks."

"What?" he exclaimed.

"Fifty. Five-zero. Five times ten. Sawbucks. Dollars. *Dinero.*" I held the Grant up to the light to check the watermark. It was real.

Dru definitely got a bigger allowance than I did.

Then I groaned. "I have to tell my father."

"Are you kidding me?" Louis said as we made our way downstairs. "This is the biggest tip we've ever gotten!"

"But—"

"We don't say anything!" He grabbed me by the shoulders. "Look, if word got out that we can't stay bribed, next time we could find ourselves in a block of cement at the bottom of the Banana River! Don't forget that guy from the InterContinental!"

"That was thirty years ago!"

"You're totally missing the point," he began again. "Look, the Tanakas aren't complaining about the TV, and if something happens, she said her parents will replace it, right?"

I paused at the top of the bridge over the koi pond and looked down at the fish swimming into the shade. Louis had a point. Finally, I let out a breath. "Okay, I won't say anything. For now."

When we got back to the main building, Dad was standing in the lobby, staring at the wide-screen TV that hung on the wall across from the check-in desk (identical to the one now lying in pieces in the Apollo Suite). Usually, we just kept it on the Weather Channel or NASA TV launch news or cycling through a video on motel amenities (Tiki bar! Hand-churned ice cream! Legendary launch parties!). Now Dad was flicking through channels, which were all fuzzy and out of focus, with patches of snowy interference.

"Not a word," Louis murmured in response to my glance.

"What's going on?" I asked.

"Every television in the motel has gone crazy," my father answered. "The satellite people said they were going to send someone out, but it could take a while." He gave us a dry look. "Mrs. Fleance wants to know if the problem will be fixed by tonight, because she wants to record *Wheel of Fortune* on her DVR."

# 3

kept us too busy for me to grill Louis on the whole wrist-bands-of-the-alien-apocalypse thing, but finally we headed out to the pool to set up for the launch party.

A pair of flat screen TVs was positioned so the guests could watch all the prelaunch stuff. At the time of liftoff, they could go farther out onto the beach or even take a float out into the ocean for a better view. Most people, though, stayed close to the pool and the food and drinks.

By the time we got out there, the three Williams grand-children (room 4-207) had already grabbed the Alvarez twins (room 3-210), and all five were splashing around in the deep end. Their grandparents were keeping an eye on them by parboiling themselves in the hot tub. Mrs. Fleance and Mrs. Jones, wearing AesProCorp sun visors, were seated at a table under an umbrella, concentrating on an intense game of gin rummy. A younger couple I didn't recognize were off at the far end playing shuffleboard.

I opened the door to the bar hut, grabbed Louis, and dragged him in. "Okay, now, are you finally going to tell me what's going on today?" I held up my arm. "Magic wrist-bands? Really?"

He took a breath and then let it out. "Kurt186."

"What?"

"On the UFO Boards," he explained. "Kurt186 gets some great info from . . . well, from top secret sources."

I wiped sweat off my face. "Do you have any idea how crazy that sounds?"

"No, really," he insisted. "He got some inside stuff from Baikonur, and then . . . Did you know the last launch from Kwajalein was held up thirty hours because of mysterious lights in the sky?"

"Umm, no."

"Well it was, and Kurt186 thinks something might be afoot for tonight, too!"

"Afoot?" I asked. By this time, my shirt was sticking to my back, so I unlocked the sliding shutter over the bar area and lifted it up for fresh air.

"That's the way he talks," Louis answered, blinking in

the light. "He's a graduate student or something in Germany. His family has some kind of major governmental connections, so he always gets good intel." He lowered his voice. "Look, I don't know if these wristbands are good for anything, but I think he might be here tonight, and if he is, he'll be wearing one of these, too!"

"Wonderful." I grabbed a rag to wipe down the counter. "Now I'm in a cult."

Louis ignored me, gnawing his bottom lip. "Really, though, if we could get away from here and closer to the launchpad . . ."

"But you've been banned from the Visitors' Center," I put in.

He scowled. "The Causeway—"

"Will be packed by now," I finished. I almost laughed at his expression. Then I quoted the new motel brochure. " 'Join us at the historic Mercury Inn and Suites for the best beach view of launches on the Space Coast.' Besides, we're being paid. Well, you are anyway."

Louis made a growling noise, but then nudged my arm. "There's Miss Gadget."

I turned to watch Dru come down the stairs from the suite. Her hair was still pulled back in a ponytail. She was wearing the same black camouflage pants and SeaWorld

T-shirt she'd had on that morning. As soon as she reached the pool deck, she opened a gigantic orange-and-blue umbrella.

"What's with that?" Louis asked as she walked over.

Dru nodded a greeting. "Even in June, exposure to UV light in Florida can cause skin lesions, which can result in cancerous melanoma later in life."

"But vitamin D is good for you," I said.

She looked pained. "I drink milk. It's vitamin fortified. Can I help?"

"Sure," I replied, even though she made me nervous. "Why don't you bring that table over here? Louis and I will—"

"I would rather not set this down." Dru gestured with her umbrella. "Perhaps if I were to . . ."

"You can't use sunblock?" Louis put in.

"Allergies," she replied, "which are signs of a hyper-active immune system rather than a deficient one."

"Fine, then," I said in a rush. "Dru, why don't you sit here? Louis and I will get the chairs."

Dru pulled out a bar stool and positioned herself under the bar awning. Meanwhile, Louis and I set to work arranging the furniture.

"She looks like a big orange-and-blue University of Florida mushroom," he said.

"Go Gators," I told him.

By the time Danielle, the bartender, arrived, we had the pool area set up. The TVs were on (fuzzy pictures and all). The adult guests were lining up for drinks and snacks. About half the kids were crowded around the base of the water slide, and the rest were playing a cutthroat game of Marco Polo.

Once or twice, Louis flexed his prosthetic knee and muttered something about having it checked. It wasn't supposed to pick up interference, he kept saying. Of course, neither were the TVs.

My mother came out to the pool once and did a thorough inspection. Then she told me I was in charge, but to listen to Danielle. Which meant, of course, that Danielle was in charge, but my mom had been a little leery ever since Danielle came back from the University of Central Florida with purple hair and a nose ring. Finally, Mom mentioned that she and my dad would be in the lobby, taking care of stuff there and watching out for the satellite TV guy.

Dusk approached. Dru and I grabbed chairs near one of the televisions and tried to watch some of the launch coverage. Louis sat off to the side of us, holding his phone to his ear to listen to Launch Control on NASA streaming radio. He said it was better than the fluff coverage on

TV. Since they had the same audio feed, I wasn't so sure, but I've learned with Louis that sometimes it's best not to ask.

"T minus ten minutes and counting," he reported. He shook the phone. "Staticky." He stood and walked in a slow circle. From the look on his face, I could tell the signal wasn't any clearer.

Dru and I sat facing north, up toward the Cape. There was nothing we could see yet, other than the glow of the spotlights and blinking lights from a spotter plane in the distance.

"All systems are go," Louis said, "and—"

At that moment, all the lights went out.

Everywhere.

At the motel, the TVs shut off. The walkway and room lights all went dark. An instant later, so did the pool. The other hotels up and down the beach and the Pier blacked out as well.

Whatever was happening, it looked like it was affecting the entire coast.

"My phone went dead," Louis said, a stunned look on his face. When I didn't react, he went on. "Dude, it's battery operated."

"That's impossible," I said. I pulled my cell phone out of my pocket. It was dead, too.

"Look." He pointed out to sea, where, moments before, lights from a dozen pleasure boats had flickered on the water. Now, there was nothing.

Louis took a step toward the beach, but pitched forward, his phone clattering onto the pool deck as he fell onto a deck chair. He hissed as his hands scraped concrete and his face hit one of the armrests. Then he rolled over with a grimace.

"The knee's battery operated, too," he said, wincing. He waved off my help, picked up the phone, and climbed onto a chaise, prosthetic leg stretched out in front of him.

Danielle came running around the bar and handed him a bag wrapped in ice. "Are you okay?"

"Yeah," he said.

Then I heard someone shout, "South!" and turned to look.

An object in the sky, glowing amber, was zooming up from the south along the shoreline. As it grew closer, I could make out a triangular shape outlined by lights.

"What *is* it?" I asked.

The crowd gasped as the aircraft *stopped* in midair about

a mile down the coast. Then it climbed straight up and moved forward again. As the craft came closer, we could tell that it was gigantic. Bigger than any plane ever.

"Holy—" Louis began.

"It's coming right toward us," someone interrupted.

"Uh-oh," I heard Dru whisper.

The huge aircraft arrived a moment later and hovered directly over us. Its amber glow looked more white now, and it was strangely quiet. I could make out five circular lights on its triangular underbelly.

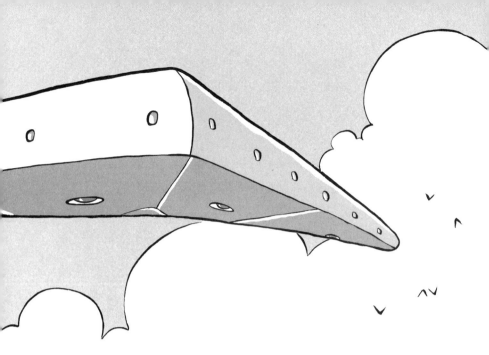

"Yes!" Louis shouted, hands in the air. "They're here!"

"It can't be," I said, but no one was listening.

The huge craft stayed there, suspended above us, for about twenty seconds. Then I felt a wave of heat, and a blast of wind blew over a pair of sun umbrellas.

A moment later, the aircraft was gone, continuing north.

"It's in restricted airspace," Louis said. He was practically bouncing with excitement despite the bag of ice under his eye. "Told you something would happen tonight!"

"What is it?" I asked again.

"It's not an airplane," Mr. Williams said, his voice tense. "Moving too fast. You." He gestured at Louis. "What's on the radio?"

"Nothing," Louis said. He shook his phone as the aircraft continued up the Cape. "The feed's dead."

Suddenly, the craft veered to the east. Then it began losing altitude in a long, graceful arc. About a mile off the coast, it plunged into the ocean.

Someone screamed.

"What happened?" I asked, my attention focused on the water where the aircraft had gone down. "Was that on purpose?"

Then the lights came back on. Everywhere. All over the motel and up and down the coast. The TVs were alive again, too. And for the first time that day, there was no snowy interference.

I shivered despite the heat. The crowd seemed stunned.

"Kurt186 was right!" Louis interjected.

"How's the leg?" I asked, only so I had something to say.

He made a show of testing his prosthetic. "Seems okay."

As he flexed it one more time, the voice of the NASA announcer on TV grabbed everyone's attention. "What *was* that?" the guy asked, over the image of the *Resolution* on Launch Pad 39B.

There came a muffled reply I couldn't make out.

Then there was another, louder, voice. "We are *not* going to tell the American people we scrubbed the launch because of an unidentified flying object!"

"Sir, we're back on the air," came the voice of the first announcer again.

Then the screen went blank. The audio was silent.

Lights were on everywhere else, though.

I glanced over at Louis. He just stood there, mouth open.

"Do you realize what that was?" he asked. "Undeniable proof that the government is out to cover up alien encounters!"

# 4

continued. "They had to have! That's why they made the exclusion zones bigger." He looked at the crowd gathered near the televisions and raised his voice. "Did anyone get a picture?"

"No," Mr. Williams said. "My camera wasn't working until a moment ago."

"It's electronic," Louis said, groaning with realization. "Digital!"

Mr. Williams nodded. "So unless you know anyone with an old Hasselblad who's still using film, there won't be any evidence."

"It's the perfect cover-up," Louis said in a rush. "It's amazing. Brilliant. A million people saw the UFO, but no one could even have gotten proof. Unless they were Amish or something. And, okay, probably there aren't actually a million people out here, and there aren't any Amish in Cocoa Beach that I know of, and they probably don't use film anyway, but who does anymore?"

"You're babbling," I told him as Danielle changed the channel to a newscast. "There's no way it was aliens! It was probably just an experimental jet. A really big experimental jet."

"An experimental jet that causes a massive, area-wide power outage?" he replied. "Come on!"

"Maybe a squirrel got into a transformer," I argued. "Maybe a bird dropped a piece of bread, like at the Large Hadron Collider. Or, you know, lightning."

"*Lightning*? On a clear night?" he pressed. "What about the TV and radio? And my leg?"

"Just because we don't know what it is," I said, "doesn't make it aliens."

"Gah!" He threw up his hands. "It's like you're dead set on not believing your eyes. And the thing was *huge*. The only way it's anything of this Earth would be if it was made using technology from the spaceship at Roswell."

With that, he pushed through the crowd to stand directly in front of the TV.

I glanced around, looking for Dru. When I couldn't spot her, I stepped forward to get a better look at the television myself.

On-screen was an image of the *Resolution* on the pad.

*Launch scrubbed due to unexplained presence of an unidentified aircraft of unknown type in restricted airspace*, the scrolling banner at the bottom reported. *No official word yet*, the text went on to read.

"Do you really think it was aliens? Why would they want to stop a launch now?" I heard a man ask Mrs. Fleance.

"What if they come back?" someone else asked at the bar.

"Never seen anything like it," Mr. Williams told his grandson.

I grabbed the remote from the bar and raised the volume in time to hear the announcer say:

"NASA officials have yet to officially comment on the scrub of the NSTS-001 mission due to an alleged unidentified flying object being sighted in the Cape Canaveral restricted airspace moments before scheduled liftoff. The object does not appear to match any known aircraft configuration.

"Speculation is running rampant. Some are attributing

it to Russian or Chinese spy planes, remotely piloted vehicles, and even extraterrestrials.

"No word yet on the fate of the F-18 observer plane or its pilot and copilot, astronauts Herb Weingard and Susan Choi."

"Wait, what did they mean by that?" Louis asked as the newscast went to commercial.

Observer jets were there to take high-resolution photos of the launch, to make sure the *Resolution* wasn't damaged on its way into space.

"It had to have crashed," I said, suddenly feeling like things had gotten a lot more serious. "It must've lost power like everything else and crashed."

Louis frowned. "This is just like what happened in the '80s."

"They scrubbed a launch in the '80s because of a UFO?" I asked. I'd never heard of anything like that.

"No, but there were reports from astronauts of UFO's tracking the shuttle in orbit," he replied. "And then in the '90s from the International Space Station. NASA tried to hush it up, but some of the astronauts talked."

"So, it's nothing like what happened in the '80s," I told him with a grin.

From the edge of the open space in front of the TV, I

looked over the crowd that had gathered to watch. They seemed to be leaning toward the idea that it *was* aliens, although a couple of folks agreed with me that it was just a government screw-up and not a cover-up.

Louis pulled out his phone and logged in to check the news sites, which he reported were running slower than usual.

A guy with a mustache grabbed the remote and began to flip channels between the local and national networks, which were all covering the story: *UFO causes delay in space launch!*

"NORAD is reporting that they haven't detected any-thing!" announced a guy sitting on a chaise with his tablet computer.

"Louis?" I asked.

He shook his head as he navigated between the national news sites.

"Look," I told him, "they're starting a press conference."

We moved in closer to get a good view, while more guests crowded behind us.

On the screen, the scene changed from the standard view of the *Resolution* on the pad to a lectern with the NASA logo behind it.

The crowd quieted as a man stepped up and began reading a prepared statement.

"Earlier this evening, the NSTS-001 mission was delayed when the launch was scrubbed due to a massive power outage that affected the entire Space Coast. NASA engineers are currently working to determine its cause, although it appears to have originated with the local Brevard County power grid."

I frowned, remembering something Louis told me once. "Doesn't Kennedy have its own generators?"

"Shh." He nodded, staring at the screen, trying to hear what the spokesman was saying.

"Minutes after the launch was scrubbed, an F-18 spotter plane and ground-based radar detected an unauthorized aircraft in restricted airspace and attempted to warn it off. As the F-18 closed on the intruder, a collision occurred, leading to the loss of both aircraft. The pilot and copilot of the NASA jet ejected and were recovered with minor injuries. No word yet on the fate of the crew of the intruder.

"Contrary to the ongoing irresponsible speculation in the media, the intruder aircraft has been identified as a specially modified B-2 Spirit bomber, testing a new wing shape and avionics platform and flying out of Patrick Air Force Base." The speaker paused. "Thank you."

Then he left, ignoring the shouts from reporters in the room.

"He's lying!" Louis exclaimed. "That wasn't a B-2! And only *one* plane crashed!"

"I know B-2s," said a gray-haired man behind us, "and that was no B-2."

"They said they modified the wing," the guy next to him argued.

"You can't modify a B-2 that much," the first guy insisted. "And it can't maneuver like what we just saw!"

"Do you know what this means? This is *great!*" Louis exclaimed, turning to me. "Okay, maybe not great, really, but for the first time ever, we totally have proof of a real-life government UFO cover-up! In real time!"

"A cover-up of what?" I demanded. "We don't have anything, other than a bunch of people saying they saw lights in the sky!"

"Look," he said, oddly patient. "The intruder object is the only thing we saw go down. Sure, maybe if the F-18 didn't have lights, we might not have seen it. But if it had lost power, it would've gone down long *before* the intruder, so why would they lie about that? How can you *not* believe your own eyes?"

I hesitated. Sure, he'd been right about something happening here tonight, but actual aliens?

He was sober now. "We owe it to the world to make sure this isn't hushed up."

# SMARTPHONE USA NEWS FEED

**TRENDING NOW**: *space clipper, UFO, launch, power failure, SETI, alien invasion, chase plane*

## HEADLINES:

*Power Failure Scrubs Clipper Launch*

*UFO Sighting over Cocoa Beach, Launch Canceled*

*Air Force Jet in Restricted Airspace Causes Delay in* Resolution *Launch*

*Midair Collision above Cape Canaveral, Clipper Unharmed*

# 5

THE CROWD REMAINED FESTIVE, AND THE
guests hung around later than usual. Everyone was hoping, I guess, to hear some official word on what had happened.

Eventually, most of the people gave up and cleared out. Mrs. Fleance, Mrs. Jones, and a few others headed inside to watch the lobby TV, away from the sand fleas.

My dad called me on my cell phone to let me know Louis's sister was there to pick him up. We left Danielle in charge of the stragglers and headed into the lobby.

As we skirted the koi pond, Louis held up his arm. "Did you see anyone else wearing a wristband?"

I hadn't actually been looking, but I wasn't going to tell him that. "No."

"Me neither."

When we got to the front of the motel, Erica was leaning against the front fender of her Mustang in the driveway under the portico, next to the luggage carts.

"I'll text you if I hear anything more on the UFO Boards," Louis said to me before he climbed in and slammed the door shut.

When I went back into the lobby, José was on the phone behind the reception desk, typing something into the reservations computer. When he hung up, he said, "It's crazy! Everyone in the world is making reservations!"

"For when?" I asked.

"For now!" José said. "They want to be here for the next close encounter!"

"You're kidding," I replied.

"We need to have UFO incidents more often," my mom said with a laugh. She came out of the office behind the check-in desk. "We're selling about seventy percent more food and drink than usual on a launch day!"

I sat down to watch the TV coverage in one of the lobby's easy chairs next to Mrs. Jones and Mrs. Fleance. At the first commercial break, a news truck pulled up in the motel driveway. A red hybrid SUV parked behind it. A short red-haired lady in a business suit stepped out, and a stocky older man with very little hair emerged from the other side.

"Is that . . ." Mrs. Fleance began, leaning around to get a closer look. "It is! It's Brita Carnegie from *One of Our Blondes Is Missing!*"

"Pardon?" I asked.

"Late night news show," Mrs. Fleance explained. "That's not what it's really called, of course, but it seems like whenever a young blond woman goes missing, anywhere in the world, they send Brita there."

I pondered that for a moment. "That's insane."

Mrs. Jones nodded. "When there was a blond sorority girl missing in San Francisco, they sent her there. When there was a blond au pair missing in Majorca, they sent her there. When there was—"

"Oh," Mrs. Fleance interrupted, "did you see the one where Brita flew her carbon-neutral Learjet down to Cancún right after the hurricane? The missing twins? That was my favorite!"

My parents were definitely going to want to get Brita's picture up on the Wall of Fame in the diner.

"Do you think she's here because of her Roswell special?" Mrs. Jones asked.

"Probably." Mrs. Fleance leaned back.

I stood to help with the luggage, if the newcomers needed it. " 'Roswell special'?"

Mrs. Jones nodded again, her dolphin earrings jangling. "About a year ago. Maybe two. Brita went out to New Mexico. She started out a skeptic, she said, but ended up a believer."

"Or at least," Mrs. Fleance put in, "she believes something happened out there that she doesn't think the government has been honest about."

"Or wants us to know about," Mrs. Jones added.

"Oh!" Mrs. Fleance held up her hand. "And she did that follow-up about the sightings last year down in Kingsville!"

"No, no," Mrs. Jones said. "It was Corpus Christi!"

"No, I'm fairly certain it was Kingsville," Mrs. Fleance told her friend.

I tuned them out as Carnegie and the man entered through the revolving door. A cameraman followed close behind.

My father stepped up. "Can I help you?"

"Yes," she replied. "I'm Brita Carnegie, and this is Dr. Horst Gleeman, and we want to do a story on local reaction to the news tonight."

"We would also like three rooms," Dr. Gleeman put in.

The phone rang. José had disappeared somewhere, so my dad had to go back behind the desk while Dr. Gleeman checked in. When he did,

Brita Carnegie and her cameraman approached me, and she introduced herself again.

"So what are your thoughts on tonight?" she asked.

The cameraman pointed the camera and light at me.

I froze. No, really, I completely locked up. I don't know why—it had never happened before. There was just something strange about the camera in my face and the fact that I didn't know how I felt.

Brita smiled with half her mouth. "Take a breath," she whispered. Then she continued, speaking into the camera. "Moments ago, we heard from the vice president—you saw it right here live. He said the mysterious object and light didn't look like any technology we have or even know about. What do you think of that?"

"I don't know," I answered. "We were on a different cha—"

"Well, what do you think of the idea of aliens from outer space?" she interrupted. "Do you think they might be dangerous?"

"Umm, I guess they could be—"

"Do you think they'll tell us we've failed as stewards for our planet?"

"What?"

"People have been saying for years that an ancient alien race has been watching us," she said, "from the skies or under the water. Do you think they're here to pass judgment on us now?"

I tried to figure out something to say. "Maybe, but why wait until now?"

Mrs. Fleance waved at Brita. "C'mon over here, Brita. Leave the boy alone."

As the cameraman focused on her, Mrs. Fleance pointed vaguely to the south and out to sea. "It was skimming along the water there, moving faster than anything I've ever seen! And then it stopped and suddenly rose up high! Came out of nowhere!"

"What do you think it was?"

"I've been living here for more than sixty years. I've seen Atlas rockets blow up on the launch pad and I was here for the first Mercury launch, and I've seen all kinds of crazy experimental planes. This wasn't anything I've ever seen or heard of before. If the vice president said we don't have anything like it, well, it's got to come from somewhere else."

"So you think it was a UFO?"

"It definitely was a UFO, but whether we're talking extraterrestrials, now, that's something else entirely. Still, if I were a betting woman, I think I'd have to say yes."

"There you have it," Brita said into the camera. "Eyewitnesses to the extraordinary events of this evening are convinced that aliens have arrived among us!"

# 6

IT WAS ABOUT ONE IN THE MORNING BEFORE
Brita gave up and went to her room. Soon after, the guests in the lobby got tired of speculating about what had happened with the launch. José shooed my parents away a half hour after that. He assured them, like he did every night, that he knew perfectly well how to clean the place up.

Our apartment was on the ground floor of the new building. It had French doors and windows facing both the ocean and the courtyard. It was nice enough, I guess. I had a room with a patio that looked out onto the koi pond. But I kept thinking—more often, recently—that it would be nice to get away from the motel sometimes, too.

At Louis's, you could swim in the pool without worrying about whether it was too chlorinated for a four-year-old.

You were never awakened at three a.m. by someone yelling that their bottles of complimentary toiletries were too small or that their pillows weren't hypoallergenic enough.

On our way back to the suite, I tried again. "You know, if we got a place off-site, we could convert the apartment into a suite. High-end. Maybe two."

"Maybe," my mom said.

"We'll talk about it some other time," was my dad's reply.

I let it drop. By the time we made it back, I was dead tired, both from the day out in the sun and the fact that I hadn't really slept all that well last night.

It wasn't just the noise from the Williamses' conga line and limbo dance. I guess I'd been feeling unsettled. Restless.

Tonight, I had the same problem, but more so.

After a while, I got out of bed. I pulled open the French doors to the patio courtyard, figuring some fresh air might help. It was warm and almost as humid as it had been during the day.

I glanced toward the pond to see Dru coming in from the parking lot. She was hauling a bait bucket, carrying a fishing rod and a tackle box. That wasn't unusual. A lot of people liked to go night fishing out by the Port or off Merritt Island. But it seemed a bit, well, off after the events earlier tonight. She was alone, without her parents.

As I watched, Dru crossed the bridge over the pond to the stairs that led to her suite. As soon as she reached the other side, she set down her bait bucket and opened the top. Then she reached in and tossed something into the koi pond.

For a while, she sat there, on the decorative rocks at the edge of the water, pulling things—shrimp, I thought—out of the bucket to feed the fish.

Suddenly, she was bathed in light from a spotlight held by Brita's cameraman.

"Good evening, I'm Brita Carnegie, and I'd like to ask some questions."

I paused in the shadows, unmoving. What could Brita want with Dru?

"The tongue of a blue whale weighs 2.7 metric tons," Dru replied. She poured the remainder of the contents of the bait bucket into the koi pond.

The fish splashed about in a frenzy as they fought for the shrimp.

Then Dru stood to head up along the pathway.

Brita blocked her way. "Please, can we have a few minutes?"

"You're more likely to be killed by a falling coconut than a shark," Dru replied.

"I want to ask you about . . ." Brita lowered her voice so I couldn't hear.

A moment later, Dru stated, "Perhaps you should go vex someone else."

Brita said something, again too low for me to hear.

At that point, I decided I had to do something. I stepped onto the pathway.

"What's going on here?" I demanded in my best I'm-in-charge tone. "Is something wrong? Should I get security?"

Brita stepped back and motioned the cameraman aside. "No need." She smiled her toothy and (at least according to Mrs. Fleance) insured-for-five-million-dollars smile. "It's late."

With a grateful glance back at me, Dru strode past the newspeople. I watched until she was up in her suite. By then, Brita and her cameraman had also left.

I waited a few minutes more. Then I went farther into the courtyard, to the spot where Dru had been feeding the koi. I approached the pond and stood in the up-lights. The koi rushed toward me, and I had the strangest feeling of déjà vu, which was ridiculous because I never fed them. Until then, I hadn't even known that koi liked shrimp.

Stooping, I spotted a shrimp tail lying on a rock and tossed it into the pond. The nearest of the fish gobbled it up, while the rest continued to throw themselves at the edge of the pond.

"I don't have any more."

After a while, the koi seemed to get the message and swam to the deeper water.

With a final glance toward the Tanakas' suite, I went back to my room.

When I finally got to sleep, I dreamt about giant space carp eating the International Space Station under the baleful gaze of an angry news anchorwoman demanding to know what had happened to the kumquats.

The next day, I woke up early to clean the courtyard. After hitting "snooze" twice, I got up, grabbed a Coke from the fridge, and headed out into the humid dark.

My parents were already up and out, of course. As usual, working in the back office and overseeing the restaurant.

Before I picked up the cleaning supplies, I stopped off in the lobby to see if anyone had heard anything more about the alleged UFO.

José, looking bored behind the desk, was surfing the Internet from his laptop.

"Any news?" I asked.

"This." He turned the screen toward me. It showed a picture of a triangular object in the sky.

"That's it!" I said. The caption indicated it had been taken and developed last night by a retired news photographer. Slightly blurry, it was the first in a slideshow of pictures that got sharper. I was no expert, but the craft looked even less like a B-2 than I'd thought.

"There's also this," José said. He clicked on a link to show a picture from the NASA Web page.

"What is it?" I asked. It looked like an airplane. Like a Photoshopped B-2.

"It's what NASA said we saw last night." He shook his head. "Scary, no?"

"Yes," I replied. Then I walked over to the lounge area to check the TV news.

A perky brunette was delivering the day's weather forecast. After a commercial, they segued into coverage of the scrubbed launch. "The Canaveral Incident," the news-people were calling it. They had a graphic of a little green man in the lower right corner of the screen.

The media still seemed to be accepting the official line. But they were showing the same unofficial pictures José had on his computer. Then they mentioned that a salvage operation was under way to recover the experimental B-2 and the chase plane.

Other than that, I didn't learn anything new. I grabbed the cleaning cart and got to work in the courtyard.

As I was finishing, Mrs. Fleance marched up, carrying an AesProCorp umbrella as a parasol.

"That pretty girl yesterday had the right idea." She saluted with it, then continued. "The café table's in the pool again."

"Pardon?" I said.

"The café table and chairs are in the pool again," Mrs. Fleance replied.

That just seemed bizarre, but I figured the Williams grandchildren were probably playing a prank of some kind. "All right. I'll get them out."

She'd stand there hovering until I did it, so I headed directly past the new building to the pool area. Unlike yesterday morning, most of the chairs and chaises around the pool were in order. Only the one café table and its two chairs were out of place. Like yesterday, they were at the bottom of the deep end.

What really caught my attention, though, was the scene out on the beach. Last night, there had been a crowd with lawn chairs and beach blankets—your typical launch-watchers. Now, there were tents. Between the time I left the pool last night and this morning, about twenty had sprung up. It looked like people were planning to stay awhile.

"What the heck . . ." I muttered to nobody in particular.

"They're here for the aliens," Mrs. Fleance said. "And for the launch, of course, but mostly the aliens. There's an Inter-net rumor that the extraterrestrials are here to send us a mes-sage and it has to do with our reaching . . ." She hesitated, frowning as she tried to think of the term. "Critical mass."

I watched a young couple start an illegal campfire in front of their tent. " 'Critical mass.' "

"Technologically speaking," Mrs. Fleance explained.

"So we're advanced enough to be taken seriously?"

That sounded ominous.

"Or to be a threat." She returned my gaze calmly. "Well, then," she added, "that's neither here nor there. Let's get the furniture out of the pool, shall we?"

With a nod, I tossed my shirt on a chaise and dived in.

I reached to grab the table. Then I spotted something small and shiny at the bottom of the pool. Kicking down, I picked it up in one hand and held on to it as I brought the table to the surface. When Mrs. Fleance took the table from me, I slipped the object into my pocket.

Within minutes, the chairs and table were back on deck, and Mrs. Fleance had her flippers on and was doing her laps.

I held the object up to the light. It was about the size of a poker chip, but thinner. Its outer edge was clear, and the interior seemed to be made of metal.

I stuck it back in my pocket and pulled my shirt on as

Brita came onto the pool deck. She was alone, wearing a red business suit and carrying a stainless steel travel coffee cup.

"Can I help you?" I asked.

She walked over, her attention still on the campers out in the early morning light. "Do you usually swim fully dressed?" She glanced at me and then at the table and chairs, still dripping water. "They were in the pool, yes?"

"Yeah," I replied. "Second night in a row."

Brita nodded. "Like crop circles."

"Come again?"

"Let me know if you find them in the bottom of the pool tomorrow, will you?"

"Crop circles?"

"There's a theory that the alien aesthetic is different from ours," Brita said, "that they feel almost a compulsion to disrupt what we perceive as order."

That sounded like something Louis would say.

"You're telling me that aliens are moving the chairs and table into the pool because they have OCD?"

"It's a possibility," Brita replied. "We can't expect their behavior to be obviously explicable. Will you let me know? The table and chairs, or anything else unusual?"

"Sure," I answered. Mostly because of my parents' mantra: Humor the guests.

# SMARTPHONE USA NEWS FEED

**TRENDING NOW:** Canaveral Incident, UFO cover-up, Roswell, vice president, space clipper, Iowa

## HEADLINES:

NASA Releases Photos of Errant B-2

Salvage Operation Under Way off Port Canaveral

"UFO Talk Is Bunk," Says Vice President

Local Farmers on Watch for Crop Circles

**FEATURES:** Southern Hemisphere Safer in Event of Alien Invasion, Experts Say

How to Talk to Your Children about UFO's

# 7

when I spotted Dru coming out of the Apollo Suite. She
waved and called down, gesturing for me to come up.

Only partly because it was my job, I did.

When I got there, Dru was sitting cross-legged on the
sofa. The television was resting on the dresser where it
belonged, but a half-dozen circuit boards were arranged on
the coffee table, with a soldering iron and a pair of long-
nosed pliers next to them.

"The term *refrigerator* was first applied to an icebox by
Thomas Moore, a Maryland engineer, in 1800," she said.

"Pardon?" I asked.

"Open it."

"Why?"

Her face was expressionless, so I walked around the counter to the refrigerator. The shelves were resting on the linoleum floor, leaning up against the cabinets next to the fridge. I paused. When I looked back at Dru, she was watching. Still without expression.

"Go ahead," she said.

I pulled the door open and jerked back, staring. I closed it again and glanced at Dru. She hadn't moved. I opened my mouth to speak, but decided not to. Turning back to the fridge, I slowly opened the door again, holding my breath as the light came on.

The object in the refrigerator had been wrapped snugly in thick, clear plastic and packaging tape. But it looked like a body.

No, it definitely *was* a body. But it was definitely not human.

It was about four or five feet long, with gray skin and arms that ended in webbed hands, or maybe flippers.

Last year, Louis told me about this thing called the Montauk Monster he said was an alien, or some kind of genetic experiment, that had washed ashore in New York. It turned out it was just a dog or something that had lost its fur because of exposure to salt water. This thing looked kind of like that, except for the eyes.

They were big and shiny, like every picture Louis had ever shown me of a little green man.

It was crammed in the fridge at an angle, resting on a case of Diet Coke, staring out toward the door.

A small puddle had collected on the bottom of the refrigerator. Water trickled out as I held the door open.

I don't know how long I stood there, gaping in utter shock. The sound of the water dripping onto the linoleum finally shook me out of it.

"What . . . is it?" I closed the door and turned to face Dru.

"His name is, was, Ishmael," she said from the couch.

"It's a fake, right?" I opened the door again, then closed it. It had to be fake. Because if it was real, that meant it was an alien. And that would mean that *she* might be an alien, too. It also would mean that Louis had been right all along.

About being visited by aliens, anyway. I didn't think he had a clue about Dru.

She placed the soldering iron back in its holder. "He's a real extraterrestrial. Or he would be, if he'd been born on our spaceship."

"Your spaceship?" I stumbled over to sit on a bar stool.

Dru's expression still hadn't changed. "I need your help. There are those who would like to get hold of Ishmael. Dr. Gleeman. Brita Carnegie. Various governmental, intergovernmental, nongovernmental, and quasi-autonomous nongovernmental organizations, both foreign and domestic."

"What is he?" I repeated.

"He's a . . . one of us," she explained.

She moved around the coffee table to stand in front of me. As I watched, she began to glow with a bluish light. It grew bright. Too bright to see through. Then it dimmed.

When the light was gone, it took a moment for my eyes to adjust.

Once they did, I saw.

Standing where short, human, ponytailed Dru Tanaka had been a moment before was a creature of about the same height and build. The skin was sleek and gray, like a bottle-nosed dolphin. Hairless, with large eyes. Almost no

nose, just slits for nostrils. A narrow mouth in the smooth face.

"You're a *gray!*" I whispered. That's what Louis called them. "Like at Roswell!"

Dru nodded. "Yes, that was all very unfortunate."

I felt my face whiten. "You're not here to . . . I mean, exact revenge or anything?"

"Relax," Dru said. She looked mildly amused. It was startling on her alien face. "We come in peace." She cocked her head. "Although, if we wished, we could melt your motel into a steaming, viscous puddle."

I swallowed. "Please don't."

"I was joking," she assured me. Then there was another flash of light, and she changed back to human form.

"Oh." I almost chuckled. "Okay." Then I did laugh. "Louis is going to *love* this."

Her expression changed to alarm. "You can't tell him! You can't tell anyone!"

"Why?"

"The fewer people who know, the better. With any luck, we'll be gone in a couple of days anyway." Dru sat back down on the couch and idly began examining the electronics again. She gestured at the easy chair next to the couch. "Have a seat."

"But what, how . . ."

"Bend at the knees and at the waist," she told me.

I moved over to the chair, but I interrupted before she could begin talking. "Wait. Are you here alone?" I stared at the human face, trying to see if I could see the alien beneath it. "How did you check in?"

"Adults of my race average about seven feet tall, so they tend not to get sent where they can interact with your people. The appearance generators can't alter the fact that they have to duck to get through your doors." She pursed her lips. "I can generate an adult-sized human persona, if necessary. But I like this one best. And it's easier if it's closer to my natural size."

"Oh," I replied. "So . . ."

"Let me explain." She looked amused and serious at the same time. "As recently as fifty thousand years ago, Mars was lush, almost completely covered with water. My ancestors arrived in your solar system and tried to colonize that planet, while your species was still trying to out-compete the Neanderthals.

"Your anthropologists would probably call us a semi-aquatic or, possibly, amphibious race, since we lived mostly underwater, in the shallow Martian seas. We still do, in fact. Here on Earth and on Europa."

"On *Earth*?" I asked.

"Yes, navigational issues in the Bermuda and Dragon's Triangles are not coincidences."

"Dragon's Triangle?" I tried to remember if Louis had ever said anything about that.

"Let me finish," she said. "Mars is a very marginal planet for maintaining an atmosphere and liquid water, both because of its size and orbit. It turned out that our colony ship—it was the only one of five to make it to this solar system—had emerged too close to Mars . . . and eventually caused vaporization of much of the water and a loss of most of the atmosphere."

I leaned forward. "How?"

Dru waved a hand. "The engine has highly localized effects on the fabric of space-time and, therefore, gravity."

I nodded as if I had any idea what she was talking about.

"So," she continued, "we fled Mars. Some of our people went to Europa, while others came here."

"Why didn't everyone come here?"

Dru hesitated. "Well, the thing is . . ."

"*What*?"

"Your people are annoying," she said in a rush. "Always have been. Even back when you were just clubbing one another over the head with rocks and sticks."

I laughed, despite how surreal it all felt.

"And you smell," she added, wrinkling her nose. "But you do have a certain kitsch appeal."

"Umm, thanks." Given that the souvenir shop down the street sold black velvet paintings of Elvis Presley and John F. Kennedy, she might have had a point. "So, then, why are you here? With a dead body?"

I still couldn't believe that Louis had been right all along.

"Overall, I would've preferred the Ritz-Carlton," she replied, "but I liked the contemplative atmosphere here better." When I didn't budge, she went on. "Occasionally, our people like to vacation on the surface. Sometimes, those who come here die." She gestured toward the body in the refrigerator. "When that happens, we have to bring the dead home before your people get hold of them. We can't let them get dissected or have their DNA analyzed."

"Why can't you just cremate him?" I asked.

She shuddered, rearing back. It took her a moment to regain her composure. "Obviously, yours is not an aquatic race."

She was silent for a long moment, so I guessed I wasn't going to get anymore explanation on that point.

"I picked up Ishmael down in Kingsville," she said finally, "but unfortunately missed my rendezvous because of a tropical storm. Oddly enough, my people have always had an interest in your space program and send a vessel to monitor every manned launch. So I came here."

I stared. "Is it usually invisible? Because I think we would've noticed if—"

"We have a technique that deflects electromagnetic radiation, including visible light, which can render our ship invisible. Occasionally there are glitches, but it usually works. We do have to turn off the device when making a pickup, however." She shrugged. "The appearance over your motel was . . . unusual . . . and a bit extravagant."

"What happened?"

"My signal was swamped by someone else's chatter." She was silent again.

"You said you needed help," I said finally. "Secret help."

"Your clipper launch will be rescheduled in three days at the earliest, assuming your people are consistent. My ship will return for it. I will need to signal them to come pick Ishmael and me up. To do that, I need to do a bit of a tune-up on my communications device to break through the interference. I also need Ishmael stored frozen, and the refrigerator there isn't cold enough," Dru said. "The body is already beginning to defrost."

"What happens if he thaws all the way?" I asked. "Or

melts, or whatever?" I walked over to open the refrigerator door. Crouching, I poked the body with a forefinger.

"He'll decompose and eventually give off noxious and possibly toxic gases," Dru replied. "In other words, your people will notice him."

"Wait, 'toxic'?"

"From what I understand," Dru answered, "some of your people may have suffered adverse effects from the Roswell autopsies."

"What do you mean?"

She shifted uncomfortably. "Their faces may have melted off."

I slammed the door shut and jumped away from the refrigerator. "Well, thanks for bringing him to a motel full of live human beings!"

"It was an accident," she replied, "and your people have come a long way with face transplants." Dru sighed. "We're a lot more careful now, too."

I decided to change the subject. "Your ship is coming back? Soon?"

"In as early as three days, depending on what your people schedule."

Frowning, I leaned to stare across the kitchen island counter at her. From what Louis had always said about

Roswell, the alien bodies had been taken away to Wright-Patterson Air Force Base in Ohio for dissection. Which I guess was true. I didn't want to think about what would happen to a live Dru if someone found out about her. "We could put the body—Ishmael—into the walk-in freezer at the restaurant. In the bin where we put the pigs for the luau. We don't have another one scheduled until next Saturday. No one should notice."

Most Saturdays at the motel, we cooked a pig in a hole in the sand out by the beach and served drinks with paper umbrellas in cups that looked like coconuts. (For those who chose the kosher option, we also served brisket.) It was a tradition going back to when my grandparents first built the place. But because yesterday was Saturday and there had been the launch party, this week's pig hadn't been touched. The alien body—Ishmael—was only a little bigger.

Dru blinked, relaxing a little. "Good."

I wondered for a moment if I was doing the right thing. If half of what Louis had told me was true, then our relations with extraterrestrials weren't all that great. But Dru didn't seem like she was plotting an invasion or anything. And it did seem like a good idea to get rid of the alien body as quickly as possible.

Dru and I headed over to the maintenance closet on the floor, around the corner from the vending machines. We grabbed the laundry cart and some fresh sheets and towels. Then we wheeled it back to Dru's room and put the body in it, covering it with the linens.

Together, we got it out of the suite and over to the elevator. When the door opened, my mom got out.

"What's going on?" she asked.

"The Tanakas want new sheets," I blurted.

She gave me one look and then glanced over at Dru for a moment too long. "I see. Perhaps I should go talk to your parents."

"They went out," Dru answered calmly.

"The two of you were in the suite alone?" my mother asked in a certain tone of voice.

"Mom!" I felt my face turn red.

Before she said anything else appalling, Mom looked at her watch. "Young man, I have to go. But you're not allowed in the Tanakas' suite unless an adult is present."

Then she left.

I said nothing as Dru and I stepped into the elevator.

"If you like," Dru put in, "I could arrange a one-way trip to the asteroid belt for her."

I grimaced. "Your parents embarrass you, too?"

"Some things are universal," she replied.

. . . . . . . . . . . . . . . . . . . . . . . . . . . . . . . . . . . . . . . . . . . . . . . . . . . . . . . . . .

We managed to get the cart across the courtyard without further incident. The plan from there was to take it to the south side parking lot, where there was an outside door to access the walk-in freezer. I, of course, had a key. The problem was to get Ishmael in without anyone seeing us.

We maneuvered the cart so that it was in the shadows of the walkway between the restaurant and Building 4. We peered out into the parking lot.

"Looks clear." I began shoving the towels and sheets aside.

"No, wait." Dru put a hand on my arm and pointed.

Parked over at the far edge of the lot, near the garbage Dumpsters, was a blue sedan. "There's someone in it."

"What do we do?" I asked. We couldn't really take Ishmael in through the front of the restaurant or even through the main kitchen service entrance.

"I have an idea. You'll know what to do," Dru said. Then she was gone, into the courtyard and up along Building 4.

I stood there waiting, feeling vaguely stupid. Occasionally, I snapped the rubber wristband Louis had made me take. After about ten minutes, though, I was getting anxious. Then I heard a loud boom, and I nearly jumped out of my skin. It was followed by a series of other bangs, sharper, not as loud. Firecrackers.

I dashed into the opening between buildings. After

unlocking the freezer door, I pulled the cart over to prop it open. I could still hear firecrackers.

How many did she have?

Pushing the towels and sheets aside, I hauled Ishmael over the edge of the cart to rest on the floor of the freezer, careful not to puncture the plastic. Or his skin.

It would take too long to drag him over and dump him into the pig bin, so I left the alien body on the floor. I shoved the cart out of the doorway, let the freezer door shut, and maneuvered the cart back into the shadows.

Only then did the firecrackers stop. I could hear voices out in the parking lot from the crowd that had gathered around the unmarked car. A cloud of white smoke dissipated in the breeze off the ocean.

"Did you get Ishmael in?" Dru asked from behind, startling me.

"Yeah," I replied, "in the freezer. But we still need to get him into the bin."

She frowned, so I explained.

We waited in the shadows in the courtyard for the crowd to leave.

"So, aquatic aliens make firecrackers?" I asked, my voice low.

She laughed. "Aquatic aliens buy firecrackers from convenience stores."

"Oh," I said, feeling dumb again. I got up to check the parking lot. The people and the unmarked car seemed to have gone.

I gave Dru a grin and unlocked the freezer door. Leading her inside, I flicked on the light and made sure the door was closed behind us.

Ishmael was where I'd left him, lying at the outside door. We wrapped him in butcher paper, hiding him in the bin with the two luau pigs. He was shaped a little differently, a little bigger, but I figured he should be able to pass casual inspection.

# SMARTPHONE USA NEWS FEED

**TRENDING NOW**: *royal wedding, plague, space clipper* Resolution, *China flooding, Salt Lake City fires*

## HEADLINES:

*Unidentified Lights Seen over Buckingham Palace*

*White House Says Vice President at Safe, Undisclosed Location*

*Yangtze River Floods; China Blames American UFO's*

**PARIS DESIGNER:** *"Green Is the New Black"*

*CDC Warns of Alien Viruses*

**OFFICIAL:** *Aliens Not to Blame for Salt Lake City Wildfires*

**WHITE HOUSE:** *"Don't Panic"*

# 8

AFTER WE GOT ISHMAEL SAFELY STORED IN THE

walk-in freezer, Dru went back up to her room and I continued to deal with all the stuff I normally did. I tried to stay as close as I could to the lobby and the diner, though, so I'd know if something happened with the body.

The TV news reported that the launch had been rescheduled for Wednesday, which meant that Dru had been right. They also reported rumors that the aliens would be returning for the rescheduled launch, which meant a lot of people were hitting the roads. Folks from up north were on their way down to see "the most important event in the history of humankind," while at the same time a good number of people down here were boarding up their houses and businesses and heading inland or even up to Georgia.

"I'm getting out until it's all over," an older guy said in an interview. "I saw *War of the Worlds*! I know what can happen!"

I'd always thought that if any aliens had been planning to invade, it probably would've made sense to do it in 1947, after Roswell, when no one was expecting it and before we had things like guided missiles and satellites and thousands of nuclear warheads. At least, that's what I'd told Louis the times he'd brought it up.

I was sitting at one of the tables in the lobby, watching the news, when he arrived. As he pulled out a chair across from me, I muted the TV. "What did you find out?"

"Nothing official."

"I figured," I told him. "That's why I turned off the TV and asked you in a conspiratorial tone of voice."

It came out kind of snide, but I was still sort of freaking out about Dru and I didn't want Louis to know. I ignored the sharp look he gave me.

"I was texting Kurt186 from the UFO Boards," he said, "and we got cut off!"

"That happens sometimes," I noted.

"We were talking about Baikonur and Kwajalein and how they're related to what happened last night!"

I tried to act skeptical, but not more skeptical than usual. "Why would anyone care enough to cut you off?"

Before Louis could answer, Dad came out of the office. "You're not going to believe this," he said, rubbing his hands together, "but we are now booked full for the next four months!" He shook his head. "We should've raised the rates."

"What?" I exclaimed.

My dad straddled a chair. "Starting tonight, in fact. Almost every ufologist, journalist, crank, and New Ager in the world seems to be trying to find a room here for the next launch." He tossed a couple pretzels into his mouth. "The last nut wanted to know if we could hold a sweat lodge, because he claims that's how ancient Indian tribes communed with the aliens. Oh, and the police are going to have an unmarked car out in the parking lot for a while."

"What?" I said again. "Why?"

"They think, since we're the place the UFO stopped over, something could happen here," he said.

"No way they're police!" Louis put in. "I bet they're feds! The government always sends out a team when something like this happens!"

With another laugh, my dad got up. "I'll leave you two alone with your plotting."

"There's more?" I leaned forward.

"I heard," Louis told me, "on the UFO Boards that top Administration officials are furious about whoever made the initial announcement of a UFO."

I hesitated, then plunged ahead with the lie. "Maybe it *was* a B-2."

"Yeah, right." He snorted. "I saw on the NASA Web site there's going to be a bunch of announcements today."

"An announcement? An announcement, did you say?" The voice came from the doorway to the courtyard. It was the guy from last night, the one who had come in with Brita Carnegie—Dr. Gleeman.

Louis's jaw dropped.

"Not a press conference?" Dr. Gleeman said.

Louis shot me a glance before replying. "Umm, not that I heard."

The man smiled. "Pardon me, my name

is Dr. Horst Gleeman. I came with Ms. Carnegie as soon as I heard about the incident last night."

"Yeah," Louis said.

Dr. Gleeman took a step closer. "Listen," he said, pulling out a business card. "Call me or text me if you see anything suspicious."

"Suspicious?" Louis asked, his tone even, as he took the card.

Dr. Gleeman lowered his voice. "Like at Roswell and last year in Kingsville." He paused. "And your names are?"

"Aidan," I said. "Aidan Caruthers. This is Louis Marino."

"Ah." Dr. Gleeman straightened, smiled, and strode to the front desk.

"Wow," Louis said, gesturing with the card. We got up and went out to the courtyard. "Do you know who that was?"

"Dr. Horst Gleeman," I replied. "He came in last night with Brita Carnegie."

"*The* Dr. Horst Gleeman," Louis answered. "He's the world's biggest expert on the Roswell Conspiracy and xenobiology and UFO's. And he's brilliant. He lurks on the UFO Boards a lot, but almost never says anything."

"Him?" I said as we paused to look down at the koi.

"He has an *equation* named after him," Louis told me. "He used to be a math professor at the University of Chicago."

"What did they do, kick him out because of his UFO theories?" I asked.

Louis hesitated. "Yeah." He hopped up to sit on the deck railing that overlooked the koi pond. "But that's not the point."

"Which is what?"

"Which is that he doesn't come unless it's an alpha level event."

"Alpha level. Is that, like, an alien invasion? When, exactly, was the last one we had?"

"No," he said, sounding annoyed. "It's undeniable, irrefutable proof that we are not alone."

"So in other words," I put in, "we should get his picture for the Wall of Fame."

"Don't laugh," he told me, then paused. "Well, okay, maybe. But this is *real*."

"Uh-huh," I replied. Then it occurred to me that Dru might've been involved in at least some of the other sightings. "What happened in Kingsville?"

"A rash of UFO sightings," he answered with a shrug.

"Some dead cows. The usual stuff." He looked back toward the lobby. "Now that I think about it, though, Dr. Gleeman was probably there. I read on the UFO Boards that NASA has been tracking something coming toward Earth from the outer solar system from beyond the Kuiper Belt."

"Let me guess," I said. "It suddenly disappeared?"

"And the government's denying it."

"Sure." I put my hands in my pockets and leaned against the guardrail. Then I frowned and pulled a silver disk from one of them.

"What's that?" Louis asked.

I handed it to him. "I found it at the bottom of the pool this morning."

"You know what this looks like?" he asked, holding it in the sunlight.

"A flattened souvenir penny from Universal Studios?"

"It looks like one of those disks of indestructible memory material found at Roswell."

"What?"

"Before the government was able to come pick up the aliens and their ship, some of the ranch hands picked up small pieces of a strange metal," he replied. "And—"

"Oh, come on!" I interrupted.

"Don't tell anyone about this." He shot a glance toward

the lobby and handed the disk back to me. "We'll talk later." Then he gestured at the pond. "That's weird."

The koi had clustered in front of us, right below where we were standing. Not just one or two; the entire school.

"They think we have food," I said.

At that moment, Dr. Gleeman came out the door into the courtyard, carrying a pair of oversized suitcases. He set

them next to a banana tree. "Boys, could you give me a hand?"

"Sure!" Louis sprang to grab one of the suitcases. "What's in these, bricks?"

"Equipment," Dr. Gleeman answered.

I took the other suitcase, and Dr. Gleeman returned to the lobby for another, smaller bag.

"What's the equipment for?" Louis asked when he got back.

"I'm monitoring some very strange signaling from the outer solar system," Dr. Gleeman said. "I'm over in room"—he looked at his key—"2-215." He led the way across the plank bridge to Building 2. "We're trying to communicate with the aliens, but first we need to see if we can detect any electromagnetic anomalies if the UFO shows up again."

"You mean like TV interference?" Louis put in from behind.

"No," Dr. Gleeman said. He looked sheepish. "That was due to leakage from my equipment." He lowered his voice. "It's not exactly FCC approved." Then he went on. "I mean the power failure. Identifying its source could lead to insights into alien technology."

"Oh," Louis said.

"And with these"—he hefted his bag—"we can signal them and monitor the entire anomaly."

While we walked, he peered back at Louis's prosthetic over the top of his glasses. "What happened to your leg?"

"Shark attack," Louis lied, like he usually did when people asked him that question. "Are you saying you've been in contact with the aliens?"

"Oh, no," Dr. Gleeman answered. "Nothing so dramatic. At least, nothing more than sending back some mysterious signals we've heard from various previous encounters. Little more than random signals, really. But with Ms. Carnegie's help, I think I will be able to send something more coherent before long."

Louis and I paused while Dr. Gleeman opened his door. As soon as it was unlocked, we entered and brought the suitcases in.

"Thank you, boys." Dr. Gleeman handed me a five-dollar bill for helping with the luggage. "Later, when I've got this set up, I'd also like to ask some questions about what happened yesterday. Is that all right?"

"Sure, anytime," Louis replied.

As we raced down the stairs, I saw Dru Tanaka sitting cross-legged in the shadow of a cycad in the garden, staring up at us.

Louis nudged me as we made our way to ground level. "I think she likes you."

"Umm." I felt myself blushing.

"Really," he said.

"Shut up."

Later that afternoon, my parents assigned Louis and me to scrub the greasy film left by waterproof sunscreen off the sides of the pool and the hot tub. So when Dr. Gleeman came down, carrying a laptop computer bag over his shoulder and a camera in his hand, we were happy to take a break.

This time, Dr. Gleeman was wearing khaki shorts, a short-sleeved shirt, and a pith helmet. On his wrist next to his watch was a silver-gray rubber band, like the ones Louis and I were wearing.

"Was it a great white?" Dr. Gleeman asked as he sat on one of the chaises next to the hot tub.

"What?" Louis replied, while I scrubbed the edge.

"Your leg," Dr. Gleeman said.

"Umm, yeah," Louis said. I bit back a laugh. Usually, people didn't ask for details. "Took it off in one bite. I was surfing the Banzai Pipeline."

"Well, then." Dr. Gleeman was silent a long moment. "I've got a business proposition, well-suited for a pair of energetic lads such as yourselves."

"Oh, yeah?" Louis wiped sweat off his face and stood to grab a bottle of water from a nearby table.

"On the UFO Boards, you are LQuatorze, are you not?" Dr. Gleeman asked.

Louis coughed, spitting out water. "How did you know that?"

"I did not, until now," Dr. Gleeman said, gesturing at Louis to come closer. "But I founded the UFO Boards to find curious and intelligent people who can keep an open, critical mind to the truth, as a tool in the quest for extraterrestrial life. People whose commitment I have seen and I can trust."

"Okay," Louis said, looking skeptical.

"And you are, in fact, the boy who was in the accident

several years ago that occurred after the spheroid sighting? Louis Marino, that is your name, yes?"

"Umm, yeah," Louis replied, somewhat to my surprise. He shifted uncomfortably, but I couldn't tell if it was because he got caught out in the lie about the shark or because Dr. Gleeman had made the connection about the UFO.

"There was no shark?" Dr. Gleeman pressed.

"Not really. No." Louis shook his head.

"Well, then," Dr. Gleeman said again, "I have a tool that I believe will help us greatly in the quest to prove the existence of alien life. I think it will be of interest to you." He booted his laptop computer and then turned on the camera. Panning around with it, he pointed it at Louis. "Very nice."

"What?" Louis asked, taking a seat on the chaise next to Dr. Gleeman. I stayed where I was in the hot tub, raising my feet to rest on its seat.

"You are human."

"I've been that way all my life," Louis replied.

Dr. Gleeman's eyebrow flicked up. "This," he said, panning around the pool area, "is an infrared or thermal-imaging FLIR camera. It has a false color mode that shows hot objects as red and cooler ones as orange and yellow and blue and so forth."

"So you can see how hot stuff is?" Louis asked, glancing

at the camera. It had its own screen, but the picture that appeared on the computer was bigger. From where I was, I could see that the hot tub showed up clearly in red. Vapor rising from it was also red.

"More than that," Dr. Gleeman replied. "With this, I can easily see differences in body temperatures and therefore identify the extraterrestrials who are living among us."

"Living among us?" Louis's voice went up a notch.

Dr. Gleeman pointed the camera at him again. "You're definitely human." He pressed a button, took a picture, then showed it to us both. Louis's image was mostly red, with orange and yellow around the edges. His prosthetic was a cooler green, except the motors. Next, Dr. Gleeman took a shot of me and then panned the camera around the pool deck again. A couple were sunning themselves on the far side, while four kids were playing in the shallow end. "They, too, are human." He looked at me. "As are you."

"Extraterrestrials are *living* among us?" I asked, leaning forward, because it sounded like something I would say if I didn't already know that extraterrestrials were, well, living among us.

"Oh, yes." Dr. Gleeman continued to pan the camera around, this time at the tents on the beach. "They disguise themselves, but their body temperature is different from ours, so we can use this to identify them. They'll show up as a different shade, slightly cooler, probably mostly orange, rather than true red."

"How long have they been here?" Louis asked. "You've seen them? With that?"

"We had some other equipment that gave us promising indications, but nothing definite," he said. "This is state-of-the-art. We believe that their first attempt in the modern era was Tunguska in 1908, but they really didn't establish a foothold until 1947."

"Roswell," Louis said.

"Yes." Dr. Gleeman looked at his watch. "Now then, I said I had a business proposition."

We waited while he blotted his forehead with a handkerchief.

He held out a twenty-dollar bill. "I would like you to take this infrared imager and take pictures of the people here at this motel."

"You think there are aliens here, at the motel?" I tried to keep my voice steady and remain calm. "Now?"

"Very likely," Dr. Gleeman said. "So I am trying to scan as many of the occupants as I can. But I am well-known and too conspicuous for this job. Ms. Brita, whom I have been working with informally, is also. However, you should have no problem and, more important, you are believers. So I will pay you boys twenty dollars a day to take pictures of the guests and identify them by name and room number. Do we have a deal?"

After a moment, I decided to say yes because, no matter what, it would be better if that camera was in our hands than anyone else's.

"Fifty bucks a day," Louis put in before I could accept. "Plus expenses."

Dr. Gleeman pulled out another twenty and a ten. "Very good."

Louis took the bills and the camera. "I want credit for whatever we discover."

Dr. Gleeman flicked his fingers. "Of course."

"Good," Louis said.

I decided to see if I could find out about the rest of why Dr. Gleeman was here. "What exactly was the other equipment you brought?"

"That," he replied, "as I said earlier, was high-powered signaling equipment. We are going to use it to generate certain coding algorithms we believe the aliens can understand. Ms. Carnegie is allowing me to use the satellite truck as a transmitter.

"Now, if you'll excuse me, I have some work to do before I see her today."

"Wait," I said, standing with him. "What are you going to do if you actually *find* an alien?"

"We shall see." He shook an index finger at Louis. "Use your wit, but be discreet."

With that, Dr. Gleeman strode off.

Louis stood there a moment, looking at the camera, at

the pool area through the viewer. He pointed it at me. Then he showed me the picture. On the screen, the heat vapor from the hot tub rose like smoke, obscuring my dim figure, which blurred into a big blob of red.

"This," he said, "is awesome. We are totally on the inside track to proving the existence of extraterrestrials."

# SMARTPHONE USA NEWS FEED

**TRENDING NOW**: clipper countdown, Navy task force, Buckingham Palace, presidential address, Cocoa Beach motel

## HEADLINES:

President to Record Greeting for Aliens

Royal Family Safe: Lights over Buckingham Palace "Just Fireworks"

F-22 Squadron Arrives at Patrick AFB for Previously Scheduled Training Exercise

Navy Task Force on Station off Space Coast

**ANALYSIS**: President Sending Wrong Message

Is This Payback for Desecration of Alien Bodies at Roswell?

## 9

move quickly.

"I need to get more sponges," I told Louis. "And soap. Something abrasive. This stuff's not coming off."

He looked at me like I'd grown a second head, but I rushed off toward the pool house. There, I closed the door behind me, pulled out my phone, and called up to the Apollo Suite. Dru answered on the first ring.

"*Moshi moshi*," she said.

"What?"

"Never mind. Is this Aidan?"

"Yeah, look," I told her. "Louis is working for Dr. Gleeman. He's got this camera thing that can detect if you're an alien, so you have to stay in your room and out of sight."

"Slow down and take a breath," she said.

I explained to her about Dr. Gleeman and Louis and the FLIR camera.

"I'll keep that in mind," she said, and we hung up.

As I put my phone back in my pocket, the door to the pool house opened, startling me.

"Dude, calm down." It was Louis. He gave me a sly look. "Having a secret talk with Dru?"

"Umm, err, well . . ."

He laughed. "Come on, we still have work to do."

By three o'clock, every last room was booked for the next seven months. At least.

The side street north of the motel that dead-ended onto the beach was packed with television satellite trucks. There were more media now than when shuttle launches had resumed after *Columbia*. Or so my parents said.

After the pool, Louis and I spent a good part of the rest of the day cleaning up a four-foot-high sand castle on the coffee table in room 1-220 (don't ask). As soon as we got back to the lobby, we were put to work helping guests carry their luggage up to their rooms. We also made sure the pool and courtyard stayed clean.

The new guests seemed to be media types, science fiction

and UFO conspiracy buffs, and plain tourists. Most of the people in the first two categories were lousy tippers and had brought so many computers that my parents were worried about whether there was enough bandwidth on the Wi-Fi network. Almost everyone—even the ones performing investigative journalism and UFO research by sunning themselves by the pool—seemed to have brought a phone or a tablet.

That afternoon, I took a breather with Mom and Dad at a table in the lobby. They were talking about whether we should get a couple of interns from UCF for the summer to help with the sudden rush of guests.

I leaned the chair back on two legs. I was debating whether to mention that we could probably move out that much quicker if we did.

Then my mom announced, "I think the luau pigs are getting bigger."

I slammed my chair back down. "I beg your pardon?"

"Marcia and I took one out of the freezer to thaw." She shrugged. "It seemed larger than usual. We'll probably need to allow a little longer for it to cook, too."

Ishmael! Obviously, though, she hadn't unwrapped him, so he was still safely disguised.

I tried not to sound desperately interested. "We're having a luau? Why?"

Mom was looking at me funny. "We decided that with all the extra guests and attention for the launch, we'd do the party up even bigger than usual. Besides, I think we're going to need the extra food."

"If that's all right with you," my dad put in with a grin.

I sat still, trying to think it through. "Taken out to thaw" meant that Ishmael was still in the kitchen. He was either on the counter or, more likely, in the refrigerator. Regardless, Dru and I needed to get him out of there. Quickly.

I was running over the possibilities when the lights flickered and went off.

A second later, they came back on again.

"What was that?" I asked as the phone rang.

Dad grimaced and picked up. "I'll check right on it," he said after a moment. He put down the receiver and looked over at Mom and me. "Power's out in room 2-215."

"Wait. Isn't that Dr. Gleeman's room?" I asked.

"Is it?" Dad strummed his fingers on the counter. "You go see what they're doing. I'll check the circuit breakers."

I hesitated outside the lobby door. Dru and I needed to move Ishmael somewhere really cold. But I didn't want Dr. Gleeman getting impatient, coming out, and discovering us with the body.

I ran through the courtyard and over the wooden

bridge. When I knocked and went into room 2-215, Brita Carnegie and her cameraman were there with Dr. Gleeman.

He had one of the standard rooms, with two full-sized beds, a dresser with a television atop it, a small desk and chair, and an armchair and ottoman. The only windows faced the courtyard and the walkway. With the air-conditioning off, the room felt stuffy, so I left the door open.

As my eyes adjusted to the dim light, I could make out Dr. Gleeman sitting in the chair. His feet were up on the ottoman, his fingers tented. Piles of equipment were stacked on the desk and on the floor next to the desk. Wires ran from some of it to a laptop computer.

"What happened?" I asked.

Brita sat on the bed. "Dr. Gleeman was trying out some of his equipment and blew the fuse."

"My dad's checking the circuit breaker," I said as the lights came on. For a moment there was the whiny hum of the air conditioner. Then Dr. Gleeman stood and began tinkering with the pile of equipment again. "You might not want to turn that on again."

"Next time," Brita said, "we'll use the generator in the news truck."

Dr. Gleeman turned to me. "We were very close."

"Close to what?" I asked.

Dr. Gleeman didn't answer. He just fumbled with dials and pressed a couple of buttons backlit with glowing lights. Then he sat down at the computer to type.

Trying to see what was on the screen, I approached the equipment. I decided it would be suspicious not to ask. "What are you doing?"

"We're attempting to detect signaling from the UFO," Dr. Gleeman replied. "N-dimensional incursions due to the UFO's hyperspatial propulsion cause electromagnetic interferences, which we can detect and pinpoint. And then send messages back."

I had absolutely no idea what he was talking about.

"Is that what happened last night?" I asked.

But Dr. Gleeman had turned his attention back to the equipment.

Brita hesitated, then lowered her voice. "He believes that it was a ship from an ancient civilization with hidden outposts across our solar system."

"Outposts?"

"Mars, the moon, and Europa," she answered, "and formerly on the dwarf planet that now makes up the asteroid belt. We'll be discussing all this and more later on the program."

"Ms. Carnegie!" Dr. Gleeman scolded. "Please!"

With an apologetic shrug, she gestured at me to leave.

As she did, I looked back at the round table that sat under the overhead fixture next to the window. Arranged on it was a pile of five small, silver disks, like the one I'd pulled out of the pool that morning.

"What are those?" I asked.

"You recognize them?" Dr. Gleeman said.

"You've seen them before?" Brita asked at the same time.

Both were now staring at me.

I shook my head. "No. I collect coins. Are those the new euros?"

Dr. Gleeman frowned down at his equipment, and Brita ushered me out.

I walked past a few rooms and took a moment to lean on the rail overlooking the courtyard. Danielle was already stationed at the wine bar. Two of the café tables were occupied, as well as the four stools at the bar itself.

I wondered what Louis would make of the fact that Dr. Gleeman had some of those disks. And why? What were they for?

As I continued on, I saw Dru watching the whole place from beside the koi pond in the shade. The koi were crowding the pond wall next to her, thrashing the surface of the water.

Then it hit me: she was right there, out in the open. Was she crazy?

I looked around but didn't see Louis anywhere. As I raced down the stairs, I noticed Dru had arranged another pile of white shells in a pentagon around her, like she'd done the day before.

"What are you doing out here?" I demanded as I came to a halt, sweating and breathing heavily.

"Meditating." She arched an eyebrow. "Or at least I was."

"Louis—"

"He was out by the pool," she answered calmly. "Next to the bike hut. I saw him before I came down."

I took a deep breath. She should be okay then. At least for the moment. But there was the other problem. "We have to get Ishmael out of the kitchen because my mom thinks he's a pig for the luau. She set him out to thaw."

For a moment, Dru was silent. "We'll get him tonight."

Which, for the second time in as many minutes, was almost exactly the opposite of what I expected her to say. I glanced around, making sure no one could overhear. "Are you *crazy*? He's sitting there unguarded—"

"He'll keep," she interrupted. "For the moment. We can relocate him tonight. He'll still be mostly frozen. We can't do anything about it now anyway. There are too many people around."

She looked up at Dr. Gleeman's room.

# 10

LOUIS WAS STARTING TO BUG ME. IT WASN'T

LOUIS WAS STARTING TO BUG ME. IT WASN'T that he was being a jerk or anything. It's just that half the time he was supposed to be working—helping me water the plants around the courtyard and whatever—he was taking out that FLIR camera and pointing it at the guests.

Most of them ignored him, but a few gave him funny looks, and I thought one or two were seriously thinking about punching him in the face.

At the moment, he was holding on to a hose in one hand and panning around with the camera with the other.

"Put that thing down!" I finally said. "You're bothering the guests. And you look like a freak."

He gave me a dirty look and dropped the hose.

Then he climbed the bridge over the koi pond, so that he was in the center of the place, and panned the camera around 360 degrees, trying to capture as many of the guests as possible.

There were already a lot of reporters and tourists hanging out at the bar and patio. A couple of families were leaving their rooms and heading out toward the pool. None of them had shown up in the viewer as anything unusual. Just normal, ordinary humans going about their normal, ordinary human business right after we were visited by aliens from outer space.

I decided to let Louis be, even when he went out to the parking lot and shot pictures of the guys in the unmarked car.

"All normal," he reported when he came back. "Well, at least as normal as guys wearing suits and sitting in a motel parking lot in Cocoa Beach in the summertime trying to look inconspicuous can be."

With that, he wandered over to the other side of the koi pond, while I turned the hose on the banana plants.

I was trying to keep an eye on Louis when Mrs. Fleance walked up to me from the other direction. "Excuse me, could you spray me a little?"

"I beg your pardon?" I asked.

"Just hose down my feet to get some of the sand off before I go back to my room."

"No problem." As I turned to spray her feet, I glanced

up and saw Dru Tanaka on the walkway of the new building, carrying an ice bucket and heading toward the door to
her suite.

I gasped and looked over Mrs. Fleance's shoulder, trying
to figure out where Louis was. Then I spotted him, standing at the foot of the bridge, pointing the FLIR camera.

Directly at Dru.

I jerked the hose, splashing Mrs. Fleance in the face.

"Sorry," I muttered at her protest, dropped the sprayer,
and edged my way past. "Louis!"

I hurried off toward him at not quite a run, hoping he
hadn't taken a reading yet. But by the time I got close enough
to see his face clearly, he was staring openmouthed at the
closed door of the Apollo Suite. Which Dru Tanaka had just
entered.

"Dru," he said when I approached, "is an alien."

"No way."

"That's what I thought, too." He sounded stunned.
Turning on the camera viewer, he held it out to me. "See,
she shows up as three degrees cooler than normal humans."
When I didn't say anything, he continued. "Dr. Gleeman
was right! There *are* aliens living among us, and she's one of
them, and she probably had something to do with the visit
last night. What are we going to do about it?"

"Maybe there's something wrong with the camera," I said, desperate now.

"No, look." He began clicking through images and speaking rapidly. "At first, I didn't believe it either, because she was in the shade and I didn't know how much that would affect anything, but then I focused on this very sunburned couple with a toddler wearing Mickey Mouse ears who were in the walkway between buildings and they looked different. Redder. So I double-checked that I had the camera on 'record' and got a couple more pictures of Dru before she made it into her room.

"And in each of them, she's different from anyone else. Cooler. Which means she's not from around here, and that means that Dr. Gleeman is right, and I have absolutely no idea what else it might mean."

"What are you going to do?" I asked carefully.

He laughed. "I think . . . I'm not sure."

I took a deep breath, trying to figure out something to say.

Louis was giving me a kind of funny look. "You *knew!*" he exclaimed. "You knew already, didn't you?"

I hesitated, then made a decision. "Follow me."

"Wait, where are we going?" he demanded, trying to catch up.

We ran up the stairs of the new building toward the Apollo Suite. I knocked on the door and opened it as Louis arrived right behind me.

Dru was sitting on the couch, tinkering with a black box, when I announced, "He knows. We have to tell him everything."

For a moment, Dru sat absolutely motionless.

"We may need his help anyway," she said finally, and stood.

Meanwhile, I moved to lock the door, then leaned against it to stop anyone from entering. Or leaving. "You can't tell Dr. Gleeman or anyone," I said to Louis.

With that, Dru began to glow with a bluish-white light and, an instant later, was transformed into alien form.

"You're a *gray*," Louis whispered.

"That's what I said," I put in, kind of amused despite the situation.

"Take me to your leader," Dru said.

"This is incredible," Louis whispered, a big grin spreading across his face. Then he started babbling, like he had to get an immediate answer to every question he had ever had about aliens. "How long have you guys been here? Was Roswell the first time you came? No, what about the Mayans and Aztecs and ancient Egyptians? Or was it the Toltecs? I—"

Dru laughed. Then she glowed white again and transformed back into normal, human-looking Dru Tanaka.

"She needs our help," I told Louis, coming forward to perch on the arm of the couch.

"Help?" he asked, and dragged over one of the bar stools.

"I'm trying to get back home," Dru answered with a faint smile.

"That's what happened yesterday," I put in, which still really didn't make any sense at all, but then Dru started to explain.

"I was hoping to use one or two signal processing techniques to get through Dr. Gleeman's noise, but wasn't able to complete my modifications before the launch." She shrugged. "So I decided I'd try again when the clipper returned and went out to watch the launch with you guys."

"But why did your ship reveal itself at all?" I asked.

"That," Dru answered, "is something I would very much like to know. It's possible that whatever Dr. Gleeman and Brita were sending sounded interesting enough or enough like a distress call that my people were willing to stretch protocol a little. A lot." She sighed. "Or it could've been a glitch of some kind. Maybe the hardware, I suppose, but more likely the software."

"Wait!" Louis blurted. "You're saying that one of the

most important events in the history of humanity was due to a software error?"

Now Dru laughed. "When your people invent glitch-free software, we can talk."

I thought over what she'd said. "But that means that Dr. Gleeman would have still been transmitting when your ship arrived, right? How come he still had power?"

Dru held up a small silver disk, the size of a coin. "With these. We use these to counteract the electromagnetic interference field that our ship generates."

"That's what those are!" I exclaimed, hauling mine out of my pocket. "Dr. Gleeman has a bunch in his room. Why did I find one in the pool?"

"I tossed mine in there to get it out of range of anything important," Dru said. "I didn't want the equipment and lights and TV on the deck to be the only things still working during the blackout."

She threw herself onto the couch, legs up on the coffee table. "I need your help." She gestured at the television. "The transmitter I'm building still doesn't have enough signal power, or processing power, for that matter, especially with the interference Dr. Gleeman is generating. I also need you to keep this secret."

"You have to," I told Louis.

He hesitated. "What do you want us to do?"

"I need to get closer to the site where the ship went down," Dru said.

"This is incredible," he said again. He let out a breath, still grinning idiotically. "For years . . ." His voice trailed off, and he shook his head, back to focusing on what she'd just said. "We could take my dad's boat."

"Thank you," Dru replied.

"What about the Lock?" I asked, getting to the logistics. Louis's dad's boat was docked at their house, on a canal just off the Banana River. But to get from there to the Atlantic, you had to go through the bottleneck of the Canaveral Lock.

"If we get there just as it opens in the morning, we should be okay," Louis replied.

"Good," Dru said, "but in the meantime, we have to hide Ishmael again."

"Who's Ishmael?" Louis asked. "You mean there's another one of you here?" He looked around like he was expecting to see someone or something jump out at him.

"He's a dead alien," I told him, "who my parents are thawing in the kitchen because they think he's a luau pig."

# SMARTPHONE USA NEWS FEED

**TRENDING NOW:** mind control, Tunguska, rapture, pyramids, apocalypse, Horst Gleeman

## HEADLINES:

**WHITE HOUSE:** "Get a Grip"

Cover-up! Mysterious Lights Interfere with Ariane II *Launch in French Guiana: UFO's or Anti-imperialist Protesters?*

*Strange Object in Sky over Russian Spaceport*

**PRESS RELEASE:** *World's largest cruise ship, the* Empress of the Ocean Seas, *will have special cruise for alien space clipper launch*

# 11

SINCE WE WEREN'T PLANNING TO "RESCUE" Ishmael until later that night, Louis ended up having to leave beforehand, despite his loud and futile protests to his mother.

The new launch countdown was proceeding on schedule.

Television crews were tripping over themselves from Daytona Beach to Melbourne. Most of them were doing man-on-the-street interviews. Others were monitoring comings and goings at Cape Canaveral Air Force Station, Patrick Air Force Base, and at all entrances to Kennedy Space Center.

When he got home, Louis sent me a text linking to news reports saying that things were equally insane outside Houston's Johnson Space Center and at Jet Propulsion Laboratory in Pasadena.

All of the major US networks and most of the major

foreign ones had descended on Roswell, New Mexico, as well. Almost all were running retrospectives about "where it had all started." Others were up at Wright-Patterson and Edwards, trying to "track down the alien corpses."

Brita had been broadcasting from all over town, including the "windswept point of Cocoa Beach Pier." She was promising a "blockbuster interview with renowned scientist and ufologist Dr. Horst Gleeman."

When one of the twenty-four-hour news networks put a stage on the roof of AP Sporting Goods and Surf Shop Extraordinaire ("Hang Ten with ABS News!"), Brita asked if she could set up a couple of chairs in the middle of our courtyard. She said she wanted to bring live coverage "from the heart of Cocoa Beach's landmark Mercury Inn."

My parents told her yes because any publicity was good publicity. Especially when you didn't have to pay for it.

I wasn't so sure.

Mrs. Fleance and Mrs. Jones were thrilled.

My parents were out late that night, spending extra time going over details for the launch party and dealing with the unexpected influx of guests. Finally, though, they made it home and locked down the apartment.

Meanwhile, I was trying to decide where the best place to hide a frozen alien corpse was. We could put it back in the walk-in freezer and switch it out for one of the luau pigs. But my parents might decide we had so many guests that we might as well roast two.

That left the old ice machine by Building 1, the only one that still had a lift-open cover and bin big enough for Ishmael. Even better, no one would question why it was locked—we always put a padlock on it at night so that people didn't come off the beach to steal the ice.

At one that morning, I grabbed the keys and snuck out to meet Dru. She was up near the courtyard entrance to the restaurant, waiting on a bench near the waterfall.

"Come on," she said. "We should get this done quickly."

I unlocked the door and followed as Dru slipped into the kitchen. Making my way to the refrigerator, I moved carefully in the dark, but still managed to bang my shin on a shelf.

Dru didn't seem to have any trouble. *Big, light-sensitive alien eyes*, I thought. I didn't say it aloud.

She grabbed a stainless steel kitchen cart while I opened the door to the fridge.

The body was still there, lying on its side on the bottom

shelf, still encased in butcher paper and plastic. We hefted Ishmael onto the cart.

"It's a good thing they didn't unwrap him," Dru said.

Back in the walk-in freezer, the two actual swine were still in their bin. Together, Dru and I hauled one over to the fridge.

"Do you think anyone will notice?" Dru asked.

The pig was lumpy and shaped differently, but if you didn't know, you would figure it was the wrapping. "If they do, what are they going to say?"

I wheeled the cart over to the door. Dru went ahead, pushing it open. Then she stepped out and gestured me forward.

The cart rolled noiselessly on its rubber wheels. It was a little hard to steer over the uneven ground, though, with one hand on Ishmael and the other on the cool steel.

The courtyard looked still and quiet. We took the chance and started pushing the cart through. Then I heard voices from the pathway between Buildings 3 and 4. We froze, right next to the bridge over the trickling brook part of the pond. It turned out to be a middle-aged couple returning from a night out. The woman giggled as the pair leaned together, fumbled with their keys, and entered their room.

"Let's go," I said, and we pushed the cart again.

The ice machine was located in a lighted alcove next to a Coke machine and a snack machine. It had a steel lid about four feet long by two feet wide and a bin for the premade ice cubes.

Dru unlocked the padlock and lifted the cover before stepping back and out of the way. I tried to get the cart in closer to make it easier to put Ishmael in.

Holding the lid of the ice machine open, I slid Ishmael off the cart and had him almost in when I heard footsteps on the concrete. I turned to see two guys, maybe in their early twenties, wearing board shorts and tie-dyed AP Surf Shop Pro Tour competition T-shirts. They were dragging a cooler with them and they were both a lot bigger than me.

"Dude," the guy on the left said, "what's that?"

"A pig," Dru answered, "for the luau."

"Cool!" the other guy said. "Lunch!"

"But . . ." I began.

I exchanged a glance with Dru. We couldn't risk getting any real attention. Already, we were making too much noise.

The first guy shoved past me and hefted Ishmael out of

the bin onto his shoulder. Then the other guy scooped ice into the cooler and they were off.

"Stop them," I hissed at Dru as we watched them go.

"How?" she asked.

"I don't know!" I replied. "Use your super alien powers!"

She crossed her arms over her chest. "You probably do not want me to vaporize your family's motel and everyone in it."

By then, the guys had opened the pool gate. As they cut across the deck, heading eastward toward the beach, I had an idea. A terrible idea. But an idea.

I ran out in front of them, turned around at the edge of the pool, and yelled, "Stop!"

The one carrying Ishmael laughed as the pair kept coming toward me.

I stepped back and then heard Dru call, "Watch out!"

Then the other one gave me a shove and I was under water, in the deep end.

When I came up sputtering and hauled myself up onto the deck, the guys were almost at the other end of the pool. Then someone stepped around the bicycle hut to confront them.

"Is that Mrs. Fleance?" I asked Dru as we ran over.

"It is," she replied.

I couldn't hear over our footsteps what Mrs. Fleance or the guys were saying.

Suddenly, the tall guy dropped Ishmael onto a chaise. Then he and his friend each grabbed a side of the ice chest and ran.

As we approached, Mrs. Fleance gestured at Ishmael. His butcher paper covering was starting to look frayed and torn. "What was that all about?"

"Umm," I began, "I forgot to move the pig last night and—"

"You'd better get it back then," she said.

"Yes, ma'am."

The surfer dudes had disappeared into a crowd around a bonfire.

"What did you say to them?" I asked.

"Now, dear," Mrs. Fleance replied, "you should know better than to ask a lady her secrets." She cleared her throat. "You might want to talk to your parents about security. Things are going to get hairy over the next few days."

With that, she went back around to sit out on a chair on the edge of the deck.

"She's not one of you, is she?" I whispered as Dru and I lugged Ishmael back to the alcove.

"Not that I know of," Dru replied.

**TRENDING NOW:** SETI, Search for Extraterrestrial Intelligence, Congress, Cape Canaveral, aliens, UFO, space clipper, conspiracy

## HEADLINES:

SETI Should Be Defunded as "Moot," Congressman Says

Governor Declares Emergency, Sends National Guard to Space Coast

**ANALYSIS:** Government Should Come Clean about Roswell, Life on Mars

# 12

back into the ice machine without anyone else trying to steal him. I locked the padlock, making sure I had all the keys. I also made sure to hide the bolt cutters. Finally, to be safe, I put an Out of Order sign on top of the machine.

My parents were still asleep. Sometimes, it was a good thing that they worked eighteen-hour days.

When I got up Monday morning, there were even more tents out on the beach than there had been when Dru and I had put Ishmael away.

The café table and chairs were at the bottom of the pool. Again.

With Mrs. Fleance's help, I got them out. Again.

At noon that day, it rained toads.

Not really, although I did see a couple of them by the koi pond after the deluge. It poured on and off for about a half hour, which only made the air feel more humid and got in the way of our getting the courtyard set up for the TV show.

By one p.m., it was sunny again, and by late afternoon, the countdown clock was ticking down, both the real one at Kennedy and the fake one that Brita had set up in the motel courtyard.

My parents had given Brita a choice location: a part of the courtyard that was surrounded on three sides by the pond. It was supposed to make you feel like you were on a peaceful island, relaxing under coconut palms and amid tropical flowers.

The news desk and chairs sort of ruined the vacation-in-paradise look, but the whole display still seemed to be a draw for most of the guests. The courtyard was crowded all afternoon, and not just because a quarter of the tables had been moved to make room for the set. Guests watched the whole thing, and even stood on the second floor walk-ways, looking down at the activity.

Brita's guest for the first broadcast was, of course, the great ufologist, Dr. Horst Gleeman himself.

When showtime arrived, Louis and I got up close, on

the second floor walkway just overlooking the stage area, where we had a clear view of Dr. Gleeman and Brita Carnegie, who both appeared slightly unnatural in the bright TV lights.

Louis used the chance to scan the crowd with the thermal imager. He'd be able to get shots of almost everyone at the motel. He still hadn't picked up any other aliens, though, and sooner or later, he was going to have to give the camera back to Dr. Gleeman. And once he got it back, who knew how long it would be before he trained it on Dru?

"Good evening," Brita began. "We're here tonight with Dr. Horst Gleeman, of the National Institute of Xenobiology, and author of the bestselling *The Truth Is Here: How Electromagnetic Pollution and Government Lies Will Kill Us Long before Climate Change*. Dr. Gleeman is here to give us his views on the UFO incident at the scrubbed *Resolution* launch last weekend.

"Dr. Gleeman, the government is now saying it was simply an unauthorized experimental jet that strayed into restricted airspace," Brita said. "But the United States Navy is escorting away any news vessels that try to get close to the site of the so-called crash. And the Air Force is doing the same in the skies."

Dr. Gleeman smiled. "Thank you, Brita. At least this

time, they're not saying it was a weather balloon. Or an early rising Venus." After a halfhearted chuckle from the audience about the reference to Roswell, he continued. "The UFO sighted Saturday evening is not like anything of this earth. However, it does have the classic wedge shape that ufologists have been able to identify many times over the years."

"Many times?" Brita put in. "Aliens have been here before?"

"Oh, yes," Dr. Gleeman said. "As I said in my book, they've been here, exploring, trying to find out about us and warn us."

"Warn us?"

"Yes," Dr. Gleeman answered, shifting in his chair to look directly at the camera. "We have been pol- luting the cosmos with our electromagnetic emissions since the beginning of the last cen-

tury with not a thought to who might be out there picking them up."

"And you told us," Brita said, looking serious, "that there's a race of Martians living in our solar system that has already suffered from this . . . pollution?"

"Yes," Dr. Gleeman said. "From top secret documents that I and others have obtained, I believe the civilization on Mars was destroyed when their promiscuous use of radio and electromagnetic telecommunications was detected by . . . others. The

descendants of those Martians who escaped are coming back here to warn the inhabitants of Earth."

"So what do we do?" Brita asked.

"We heed their warning!" Dr. Gleeman said, as if it were only too obvious. "We shut down all unnecessary radio and electromagnetic transmissions that could escape the ionosphere. Throw away our cell phones and our BlackBerries and our televisions . . . return to communications that stay local to our planet."

"All right, then," Brita said with a plastic smile. "Wouldn't that be very expensive? Cause massive unemployment in the media sector of the economy? Cut down on the available radio and television channels and restrict the voice of the free press?"

"Yes," Dr. Gleeman said. "But the alternative is far worse."

"Well." Brita shifted to smile into the camera. "What about the space clipper? Why here, why now?"

"We're on the verge of returning to the moon and to Mars, and we're going to be sending an unmanned probe to Europa soon as well. We're starting to look beyond ourselves again. It's natural the aliens should come back here and check on their descendants."

"Their descendants?" Brita momentarily lost her smile. "You mean, *we're* their descendants?"

"No, don't be silly," Dr. Gleeman said. "I'm talking about the dolphins."

"Dolphins?" Brita's tone was bland.

I stared at Louis in astonishment.

"She should've read his book," he murmured. "You should've, too."

"*Dolphins* are the descendants of little green men?" Brita continued, her voice rising in pitch.

"They're more of a grayish color, but yes," Dr. Gleeman said. "They colonized us millions of years ago, and when their civilization was destroyed, some of them stayed here, some went to Europa, and they took different evolutionary paths."

"The ones here became dolphins?"

"Absolutely," Dr. Gleeman said. "And further, the evidence suggests that an early australopithecine ancestor of ours became aquatic at the same time, eventually emerging again from the seas to become *Homo sapiens*."

Brita was speechless for a moment and then a moment longer. "Thank you, we have to take a commercial break." As soon as it began, her smile fell flat. "*Dolphins? Like Flipper? Are you kidding me?*"

"Well, no." Dr. Gleeman seemed unperturbed. "Didn't you read the book?"

Brita sat back in her chair, crossed her arms, and glared.

A minute later, Brita's producer handed her a paper and gestured the end of the commercial break.

"Right, then," Brita said, sitting up and perky once more. "Let's move along to the actual encounter. Why do you think people are responding so strongly? We've seen the reports— the interstates into and out of Florida are practically bumper-to-bumper. The traffic's worse than during a hurricane evacuation. And there are reports of crowds of spectators gathering outside other spaceports around the world, as well."

"This is a transcendent moment in our history," Dr. Gleeman said, "the moment when we all wake up and realize that we share the universe with others. It is bigger than harnessing the atom or landing on the moon. Much bigger. Many people want to be here to see it so they can claim a part of it as their own."

Brita paused thoughtfully. "We don't really know that the aliens will be back for the rescheduled launch, although we expect them to be. Do you think they will?"

"I am almost certain—"

"Thank you, Dr. Gleeman," Brita interrupted. She smiled. "When we return from our commercial break, we'll be discussing what you can do to protect your family and your pets from the potential alien threat."

# 13

people showed up on the beach with camping equipment. That morning there had been about fifty or so campers. By the time Brita's show was over we'd reached hundreds, and they were still coming.

That night, I had trouble sleeping. Again. Eventually, I sat up in bed to read Dr. Gleeman's book (he'd left a signed copy in the lobby). I reached the chapter where the business of the dolphins being descendants of Martians ties in to a conspiracy with the Masons and "what really happened to *Voyager 2*" when I heard a noise in the courtyard. According to my alarm clock, it was two in the morning.

When I went out on my patio, I didn't see anyone.

Suddenly, though, I felt like doing something active, something other than sitting and reading. I put on my swimsuit and a T-shirt, grabbed my goggles, and went out to the pool. It was funny; I hadn't done a night swim like that since I was maybe ten.

For some reason, it just felt right.

The lights were dimmed, since technically the pool closed at eleven. From the beach, I could see campfires and hear voices and loud laughter. I dived in. As I approached the deep end, ready to do a flip turn, I could just make out, in the shadows, the café table and chairs. And seated in one of the chairs was Dru. I frog-kicked down and gestured to her to surface.

"What are you doing?" I asked as we treaded water. "What's the deal with the table and chairs?" I couldn't believe she was the one putting the furniture down there. What if someone had seen her?

"Amphibious, remember?" she replied.

I wasn't sure that made any sense at all, but decided to leave it at that.

"We should probably put them away," I said.

Dru shook her head. "Leave them until morning."

"Why?"

"I don't want to mess up Brita Carnegie's understanding of the 'alien aesthetic.'" With that, she swam toward the edge of the pool.

After a moment, I followed.

Then something occurred to me. "But you came out here the night of the launch. Why didn't you pick up your disk thing then?"

She gave me an intense look. "I thought it might be more useful there."

Before I could respond, she'd climbed out.

"Ishmael is secure?" she asked as I lifted myself to the deck beside her.

I held up a ring of keys that I had set on one of the pool-side tables. "The only keys. My parents won't bother with trying to open the machine unless they get actual complaints. I checked—all the other ice machines are working fine."

"Good." She slipped a pair of shorts and a T-shirt on over her swimsuit while I grabbed my polo, pulling it on as she began walking toward the beach.

I stepped into my flip-flops and followed, catching up as she reached the beachside pool gate.

The beach was covered in tents. Campfires cast eerie shadows, lighting up the sand above the high-tide mark. Most of them were lit in front of individual tents. In a few places, a group was clustered around a bigger fire, almost a bonfire. The sounds of partying and music drifted above the crashing surf.

"You sure you want to go out there?" I asked.

She stepped through the gate.

We meandered through the tents and partiers, looking at handwritten signs people had put up. FORGIVE US FOR ROSWELL! WELCOME, ALIENS! REPENT! KLINGONS FOR INTERGALACTIC PEACE!

Dru shook her head as I walked beside her. "They're all here . . . to see. Why?"

"History, I guess."

We passed by a tent with a group gathered around a guy playing a ukulele.

"Why?" Dru said again.

As a girl in a bikini dashed around the tent, we tried to

dodge out of the way. Right behind her came a guy in board shorts and no shirt. When he reached to grab her shoulder, the girl tripped, spilling her drink on Dru.

"Sorry," the girl blurted. Then she was up and off again, the guy following.

I handed Dru my towel. "Knowing we're not alone. It would change everything."

"How?" Dru asked as she patted herself dry. "This seems to me like every beach during every spring break everywhere."

I wasn't sure why the campers had all come. Any excuse for a party, maybe. But there was more to it than that. The fact that we weren't alone. It mattered.

Still. "Sometimes, humans can be jerks," I admitted.

"It's not unique to primates." Dru handed me back the towel. "Thank you."

We made our way down to the waterline, walking barefoot, where the tide was still receding. The wet sand felt cold. The lights from the hotels and condos and fires lit up the night. For a while we stood still, staring out at the ocean, breathing in the smell of salt and fish. After a while, I turned to look at her and nearly jerked back in surprise when I found her staring at me. I felt my face turn red, expecting her to laugh, but she didn't.

She turned to stare at the waves again.

"You know," she said, "Dr. Gleeman is wrong about most things, and most of what he's right about is so completely garbled it's almost tragic, but he's right about one thing."

"You mean about aquatic apes?"

"No," she replied, "about the fact that it isn't all that wise to send out your ludicrous news and entertainment transmissions into space, shouting 'Here I am' to anyone who might hear. The universe is a dangerous place."

I didn't have a response to that.

Not long after, we made our way back to the pool deck, this time without getting sprayed by any beverages. Instead, we accidentally stepped in between a group of guys from Brevard Community College. For some reason, they were throwing chunks of fried cod at one another.

When we returned to the motel, I took a quick glance at the parking lot. The blue car was gone. A black one sat in its place.

# SMARTPHONE USA NEWS FEED

**TRENDING NOW**: launch update, presidential address, Mars

## HEADLINES:

I–95 Stop-and-Go to Georgia Border, People Urged to Stay Home

Area Parks Overflowing with Alien Thrill-seekers

World War II Submarine Spotted on Mars!

Mona Lisa *Removed to Underground Bunker; "Just a Precaution," Says Museum Director*

# 14

morning, the beach was absolutely packed with thousands of campers, with barely an open patch of sand to be found. The parks up in Titusville and Cape Canaveral were wall-to-wall with spectators, too, or so we were hearing. The county was estimating that about two million people had gathered to watch the launch. Every one of them was eager to see a UFO.

The old old-timers claimed it was almost more exciting than during the Mercury or even Apollo eras.

After I showered that morning, I made my way to the lobby to see if my parents had heard anything new. I had that fuzziness that comes from lack of sleep, but also an odd adrenaline feeling that something was about to happen. Sort of like Christmas morning, but with the possibility of alien invasion. Still, I would have stayed in bed a while longer, except I needed to make sure Mom and Dad hadn't opened the ice machine.

When I got to the lobby, only my dad and José were on duty. Mom had taken the minivan out to try to pick up extra supplies since it looked like we might miss our weekly delivery. It felt a little like preparing for a hurricane, although most people hadn't boarded up their windows. Not yet, anyway.

A quick check of the Kennedy Web site showed the launch was on its scheduled T minus eleven hours hold. No new security measures had been implemented, or so they said. No sightings of anything unusual had been reported. Yet.

As I logged off, Dad gestured at the stage, which was what we were calling the area where Brita and her crew set up. "We've been keeping it tidy for the film crews. Don't want to give TV viewers the wrong impression. Check out the pool and hot tub, though."

"Will do," I replied.

I yawned. Then I exited to do a check on the courtyard. Dad was right—there wasn't much left to do. I took a quick look into the Building 1 vending alcove. The lock on Ishmael's hiding place was still there, so I didn't hang around.

The surprise came when I got out to the pool. In addition to the table and chairs, about twenty cell phones sat at the bottom, casting long shadows in the underwater lights. They hadn't been there last night.

"What happened?" I asked Eduardo. He and Jaime were standing watch at the beach side of the deck, although I wasn't really sure what they were planning to do if the horde of tourists decided to charge.

Eduardo shrugged. "The police are keeping the campers away." Then I saw what he was looking at. Two groups were clustered together on the beach. One of them held signs saying LISTEN TO THEM! and THROW AWAY YOUR PHONES! The other group had ALIENS GO HOME!

"Are cell phones toxic?" I asked. "Do we have to drain the pool?"

Eduardo shrugged again.

I stood at the pool's edge, trying to decide whether it would be easier to dive in to get the phones or use the net. I wondered when Mrs. Fleance would appear to complain. Then Brita and Dr. Gleeman came strolling around the corner of the pool bar. The cameraman walked backward in front of them, training his lens on the pair.

The instant they came into view, both crowds began

cheering and thrust their signs into the air. The anti-cell-phone people threw a couple more phones into the pool.

"We bring you a report about the crash of an F-22 earlier this morning," Brita said into the camera. "The fighter jet was on a routine patrol and suddenly lost control, plunging to the earth above Cape Canaveral. The pilot was recovered and is reported to have only minor injuries. The Pentagon has no word on the cause of the crash and refuses to comment on speculation that it encountered an alien spacecraft. Pentagon spokesman Stuart Smith notes that this isn't the first time an F-22 has crashed, but there are certainly jitters about the timing and location of the accident.

"What about it, Dr. Gleeman? Is it possible that the crash is connected to the UFO sightings?"

"Brita, obviously it's connected, in that the jet wouldn't have been here if it hadn't been for the incident of three days ago. But . . ."

I stopped listening when Mrs. Fleance nudged my arm with her AesProCorp umbrella. She nodded at the pool. "What are you going to do about those?"

"I'll get them out," I said, preparing to dive in.

"No, don't," she replied as another phone sailed into the water. "I'm not going to have you bonked on the head by those dolts. I'm taking a break, at least until the day after tomorrow."

She moseyed off to sit by a table under an umbrella.

I took in the crowd for a moment more. Then I saw Brita and Dr. Gleeman plunge into the mass of humanity on the beach. No one pelted them with fish.

# 15

"IF I'M NOT OUT OF THERE IN TEN MINUTES, call the police," Louis said.

"The police are the last people we want hanging around," I told him.

We were sitting near a trio of coconut palms on the far end of the courtyard. We had a view toward the lobby so I could see if my parents came out and we could look like we were busy. And, more to the point right now, we had a perfect line of sight to Dr. Gleeman's room.

Louis had decided it was time for him to make his report. Deleting, of course, any pics of Dru and any evidence that there actually were aliens at the Inn.

He steeled himself and marched off. I watched him disappear into the stairwell and then reappear a moment later on the second floor walkway. He knocked on the door and entered when it opened.

I sat there, watching the room and watching the stop-watch on my cell phone. Once, I spotted my mom coming out of the lobby, so I scurried behind a palmetto. When she went back inside, I saw that seven minutes and forty-five seconds had elapsed.

And that's when Dr. Gleeman, Brita Carnegie, and the camera guy burst out of room 2-215. For a second, I just sat there, wondering what had happened. Then Louis emerged from the room, looked directly at me, and waved me over with the FLIR camera. I came out of my hiding place and followed.

I thought at first that they were on their way out to the north parking lot, but to my surprise and horror, they paused in front of the Building 1 ground floor vending alcove.

I stopped in my tracks, trying to decide what to do, when Louis came up to me.

"Ishmael," I whispered.

"How did they know?" Louis asked.

A group of ten or so onlookers had already gathered to watch.

"What happened up in the room?" I asked.

"Nothing," he answered. "And then they got an anonymous phone call."

Before I could ask him any follow-ups, Brita turned around and began speaking to the camera.

"This is Brita Carnegie, reporting live from the Mercury Inn and Suites in Cocoa Beach, Florida," she said. "Dr. Gleeman and I have recently received credible information that alien bodies are being hidden here at the Inn, and that is the reason for the visitation the other night."

As Brita edged closer to the ice machine, Louis and I stayed put at the back of the crowd. I tried to decide if I should shove my way to the front or stay where I was and play innocent.

When Dr. Gleeman pulled a bolt cutter from his satchel, I moved forward, Louis beside me.

"We have reason to believe," Brita was saying, "that certain persons here in Cocoa Beach have, in fact, been secretly trafficking in alien bodies and body parts and that one such body resides here in this humble ice-making machine."

"Stop them!" Louis whispered. "Isn't this, like, vandalism or breaking and entering or something?"

"If I do anything, they'll know something's up," I said. I knew it sounded lame, but it was true. Interrupting Brita would only buy a few minutes, and my parents would probably just open the freezer up anyway, since it was supposed to be unlocked during the day.

Dr. Gleeman cut the padlock off the ice machine and tossed it to the concrete floor, where it fell with a metallic clang. Then he grabbed the machine by its side and, playing for the camera, pulled it so that it faced toward the alcove entrance. With a dramatic flourish, he opened the cover to the bin.

Inside, an object wrapped in butcher paper lay exposed to the camera.

Louis let out a loud breath.

Brita and Dr. Gleeman pulled the body up so that one end was exposed, out of the bin. Then she tore at the paper and used a pocketknife on the plastic underneath.

With triumphant grins, they stepped back, and with one hand Brita peeled back the plastic to reveal the body underneath.

We all stared. Not at the face of a dead alien. At the snout of a dead pig.

I don't know who was more surprised, me and Louis or Brita and Dr. Gleeman. We all stood there gaping while some folks in the crowd laughed, but it was a nervous laughter.

"Underneath, maybe?" a guy in a Panama hat suggested.

"Just like Al Capone's vault," an older lady wearing a Hawaiian shirt said in a disgusted tone.

Dr. Gleeman lifted the pig out a little to look under it. A moment later, he focused on me. "You! You work here! What's this doing in here?"

I froze. Then I realized I had nothing to be panicked about. This was my parents' motel, and these people had no right to be hacking away at locked cabinets. "It's a pig," I said. "We roast them for luaus."

Another giggle from the crowd.

Brita looked furious for a moment, but then it seemed like she'd made up her mind. "It must be in the cooler in the restaurant!" She marched past Louis and me and the rest of the crowd, her cameraman and Dr. Gleeman trailing behind her. The onlookers turned and followed.

"What's going on?" Louis whispered after making sure everyone was clear. "I thought Ishmael was in the bin!"

"He was!" I replied. "I didn't move him!"

"I didn't move him either," Dru answered, appearing from around the corner and startling us both.

I felt the blood drain from my face. "Which means Brita is right! If he's still at the motel, he has to be back in the walk-in!" I raced across the courtyard to the restaurant, where the group was trying to shove its way into the service entrance. I briefly wondered if Brita had kept the cameras rolling live, but I couldn't see a TV.

When we arrived in the kitchen, the crowd was there in front of us, with the camera facing Brita and Dr. Gleeman as they stood there in front of the stainless steel prep table, another pig, unwrapped, resting atop it.

At that moment, my mom stormed in from the restaurant side. "What's going on here?" She wiped her hands on her apron. "No, wait, don't answer that. Everyone out!"

Brita lowered her microphone and gestured at the camera guy to lower his camera. She gave me a long, long look as she and Dr. Gleeman pushed past the crowd to get outside.

Louis, Dru, and I waited until everyone had gone and then we slipped into the kitchen.

My mom eyed us, hands on her hips. "You have five seconds to tell me exactly what is going on here."

Which didn't seem fair at all.

"We don't know," Louis said, lying brilliantly. "I think Brita decided that the luau pigs are cryogenically frozen aliens." He shrugged. "You know how media people are."

"There are days . . ." My mother brushed back her hair. "You three, go!"

We did, but not before I glanced into the pig storage bin and the open refrigerator, which were both empty.

Where was Ishmael?

# 16

"WHERE IS HE?" I ASKED DRU AFTER WE

retreated up to her suite.

"I don't know," she replied as calmly as usual, but there was a tightness around her eyes. She perched on one of the bar stools, while Louis leaned against the counter.

"Dr. Gleeman has to suspect you're an alien," Louis said, focusing on Dru. "It's the only explanation. And someone had to have tipped them off about Ishmael."

"Can your ship come sooner?" I went behind the counter island and opened the refrigerator door. Empty. "Thought I'd make sure," I said.

"No," Dru replied. "The com device isn't working; there's too much interference."

I returned to the living room, throwing myself onto the

couch and pressing my hands to my forehead. "So, are we going to forget about Ishmael?"

"There's nothing else we can do," Dru said.

"We're giving up?" Louis demanded.

"Who could've taken him?" I asked at the same time.

"It had to have been the government," Louis went on. "The guys in the unmarked cars."

"No way they saw us put him in the bin," I said.

"They had to have," Louis answered. "And if they know about Ishmael, then they know about Dru, too. Why haven't they taken *her*?"

"Maybe they only want cadavers," she said.

"Either way, we have to get you out of here," he replied.

Dru nodded slowly. Then she turned to me. "It's time for you to go home, too."

I didn't understand. "What do you mean, 'home'?" I asked.

Dru didn't say anything for a moment. "There is another reason that I came here." She walked over to stand in front of the mirror that hung above the buffet in the dining area. "Come closer."

Unnerved, I got up and stood beside her. Both of us faced the mirror.

She touched the back of my neck.

Instantly, I felt a warm flush and saw sparkling lights. When I blinked, I was not in the mirror anymore. At least, not the me I knew.

I was a gray.

# 17

I jumped back. Then there was another flash, another sensation of warmth, and a moment later, I was me again.

I staggered over to collapse onto the sofa. "What? How?"

"You're one of *them*," Louis whispered, standing and approaching to get a better look.

"I . . . I . . ." I started to say, and my mind went blank. Completely blank.

"Changeling," Dru said, and grabbed a bottle of water from the fridge.

Louis cleared his throat. "What, you mean like elves switched at birth?"

Dru grimaced. "He could've been switched at birth, but usually, like in this case, it's much later. Some of my people trade places with humans for recreational reasons, or to better understand your species, although it's not usually considered ethical."

"Could you not talk about me like I'm not here?" I demanded.

Then I saw Louis go pale. "Wait, you mean there's another, real Aidan out there somewhere?"

"I *am* the real Aidan," I protested. "I don't know anything about aliens."

"You wouldn't," Dru said softly. "At least not yet. The body you're in is an alien body, but your soul, if you will, is that of the human Aidan. Human, physical Aidan is back at our home with an alien soul. You will be switched back, and at that point, you will have each other's memories. Both sets."

I had absolutely no clue how I felt. Or should feel. I was way totally beyond freaked out.

"Why?" Louis asked, waving his hand in front of my face. "What are they doing with him? His real body?"

"Usually, as I said, it's for recreation or research. One of our people will inhabit the human body and live among the humans. The human consciousness will live in the Changeling's body until it's time to switch back. In this case, though, something more is happening." Dru sat on the sofa next to me.

"What?" I demanded.

"The alien body you're in was also disguised as a human—like I am. But we're also able to make . . . adjustments . . . to the memory centers."

"You mean memory wipes," Louis interjected. "So people don't talk about their close encounters."

"Yes," Dru answered, without taking her eyes off me. "In this case, we removed the memory of your accident or even the Change itself. You have never been allowed to realize that a switch occurred because . . . your body is recovering." She glanced at Louis's leg. The prosthetic one.

Louis got it first. "Holy . . ." he began in wonder. "Your people *were* at the accident."

"Yes," Dru answered. "My brother was flying that craft and, unfortunately, was seen. The other driver ran the light and was killed, and you were brought aboard one of our ships."

I began, "But—"

"You, Aidan, were Changed to save your life," Dru said. "Your injuries were extensive."

I groaned.

Louis leaned back into the easy chair. "That was two years ago. Do you mean he's been in an alien *hospital* ever since?"

"His human body has been in a medical bath, yes." Dru nodded. "It's a slow process, but involves very little pain."

Before I could figure out what to say, Louis spoke. "Have you been Changed, too? Or whatever it's called?"

"No," she answered. "I just have an appearance implant. Which is another reason I came for Aidan now. Although the Change is mostly stable, the appearance implants have been known to malfunction if they've been on too long. And considering how your people react to a UFO, I don't want to think about what would happen if it gave out while he was in public."

"You were telling the truth?" Louis said. "About Changing Aidan back? He'll be okay?"

She glanced at me. "He should be. But he won't be quite the same person. We'll let him keep the memories of life with my people in addition to those of life here."

"Which means what?" we both said.

She hesitated, and I swear she smiled, even though her expression didn't change. "He'll be able to do multivariate calculus in his head."

Louis snorted, then frowned. "Wait a second. Why . . ." His voice trailed off, and he held up the FLIR camera, pointing it at me. "Last time, you were in the hot tub, so your body temperature could have blended with the steam."

He took a picture of Dru and me and showed it to both of us. We were the same color. Which meant we had the same body temperature.

That's when it all struck me.

I was me, but not me.

I'd nearly died.

I shoved past Louis and fled the room. I slammed the door behind me and ran down the walkway, down the stairs, and into the courtyard.

# 18

I WANTED TO BE ALONE. THE PROBLEM WITH THE

motel was that there was no good place to do that. There were always guests wanting something or doing something you had to clean up or fix. Even in the apartment, I couldn't get away. My cell phone was an electronic leash.

But now I didn't even know if all that was me. Real me or fake me. Human or little green—gray—man.

Walking aimlessly, I found myself out by the pool. Someone had cleared out the cell phones, and the crowd had been moved away from the deck by a police line. Beyond throwing distance.

I inhaled the salty air, felt the heat and humidity on my skin. I looked out onto the ocean, trying to ignore the tourists and the campers.

"Excuse me, are there any more towels?" asked Mrs. Cruz (room 1-109).

"Over there." I pointed to a stack next to the bar. Then I fled.

I don't know how long I wandered. I ended up on the roof of the new building. There was a spot on the ocean side and away from the air-conditioning units that had a view of the entire coast. I hadn't gone up to the roof in years. I found myself sitting there again, in the corner, knees drawn up. I shivered despite the heat, staring at the sky.

# 19

"DOES IT REALLY MATTER THAT MUCH?" THE
voice startled me. It was Dru, holding open the door to the stairs, Louis beside her. "The fact that you'll have alien memories now?"

"You can read minds, too?" I asked, not caring about the bitterness in my voice.

"No." She stepped over, facing me. She was silent, expressionless.

"It matters," I told her finally.

"How?"

"It's . . . it's . . ." I struggled to put it into words. "I'm a lie!"

She nodded. "Yes. But a lie that makes a difference?"

"Yes!" I said. "Of course!"

"Really?" she asked. "Because it seems to me that you're

you and will be the same you when you're returned. Your parents, friends, everything you've known, everything you've thought, are reflections of you, not your body. And you're alive."

I paused. Louis had lost a leg. I had lost . . . I don't know what I'd lost. "I almost died?"

"Yes," Dru said. "Eighty-three percent of the bones in your body were broken, most of your internal organs were shutting down, your brain was hemorrhaging, and your body was perforated like Swiss cheese. You are now completely recovered. One hundred percent healed. So we need to get you home. It's time."

I thought about that for a long moment. It didn't make me feel a whole lot better. But it was something, a second chance, and she was right.

"Okay," I said finally. I got up to leave.

Louis held open the door, but then his knee made a piercing screech and began to buzz.

"What is wrong with this thing?" he muttered, flexing it, still holding the door.

"Dr. Gleeman," Dru said. "It must be picking up his attempts at transmission."

# SMARTPHONE USA NEWS FEED

**TRENDING NOW**: Brita fail, Mercury Inn, Cocoa Beach, alien autopsy

## HEADLINES:

Brita Carnegie Fails to Find Little Green Men, Ratings Huge

Space Launch on Schedule, No Aliens Reported Yet

World War II Submarine on Mars Vanishes!

**THE SECRET OF ROSWELL:** The Rancher Speaks

**ANALYSIS:** Why Haven't We Heard from the Astronauts?

# 20

DRU HEADED UP TO THE APOLLO SUITE WHILE Louis and I got things ready for our plan to return Dru to her people and Change me back. We put our bicycles on standby and called Louis's mom to tell her he'd be spending the night at the motel. Hopefully, she'd be asleep when we took the boat from their dock.

Later, while Dru finished fixing her transmitter, Louis and I got a chance to retreat to my apartment for a snack.

"You okay?" he asked as we made peanut butter sand-wiches.

I was quiet a moment. "No," I said, "but I think I will be."

"Good."

Then it occurred to me for the first time.

"What about you?" I glanced at his prosthetic. "They weren't able to—"

"I asked," Louis interrupted, his tone flat. "While you were out on the roof freaking out." He grimaced. "Dru said there wasn't enough left to even begin to reconstruct."

*Mangled beyond belief,* one of the doctors had said at the time.

"Oh," I said. "Sorry."

"Yeah," he replied, and poured a glass of milk.

I gave him a long look, cleared my throat, and decided to change the subject. "So. What do you think I'm like?"

Louis cocked his head, giving me an appraising look. "From what Dru said, you'll be the same pain in the butt you are now, but you'll probably be a lot better at water polo."

"Why?"

"Think about it," he continued. "You're an aquatic species, so you probably do a lot of swimming. But you won't be able to breathe underwater anymore, unless they let you keep the gills."

*Gills?*

I don't think anyone in the motel—maybe the entire state— was planning to get any sleep. The atmosphere was intense.

Every grain of sand on the beach was now occupied by campers and spectators and newspeople.

Everyone in the motel seemed to be outside on the pool deck. They were all watching the sky or the news or surfing the Web for the live NASA feed and live blog of the countdown.

The now-thawed real pig was slowly roasting in the luau pit.

We had to get three people off the roof (they'd climbed up with telescopes and were scanning the skies, or so they said).

At around ten, there was a report that a UFO had been sighted.

At ten thirty, there was a report that the previous report was a hoax.

At ten forty-one, there was a report that the previous report that the previous report was a hoax was a hoax.

At midnight, the countdown began again from its scheduled hold.

Brita was on the stage below, chirping about the upcoming launch and the possibility of UFO's. Dr. Gleeman sat next to her.

I had one last talk with Dru, down by the koi pond, before we left. She was standing on a rock, throwing bits of bread to the fish.

"How big a deal is it," I asked, "that you don't have Ishmael?"

She hesitated. "It depends. If it's made public, a big deal. If it's kept quiet, not much. Hopefully. It's happened before."

I grabbed a handful of bread crumbs and tossed them to the gathered koi. Then it occurred to me. "Louis is right. Whoever took Ishmael has to be with the government. Otherwise, he would've already been made public."

Which meant they'd probably only dissect Ishmael instead of parading him around in front of the TV cameras and *then* dissecting him.

# 21

WE SNUCK OUT IN THE DARK OF THE EARLY
morning. I left my parents a note saying we wanted to
check out the scene at the Pier.

We met up with Dru near the storage room where we
had left the bikes the day before. She was wearing a black
T-shirt, jeans, and gym shoes, and carrying a backpack with
her transmitter.

As Louis unlocked the door, I peered between the buildings and looked out onto the beach. Even though my view
was limited, I was able to see a bunch of campfires and the
crowd of campers and spectators. No one was paying attention to what was going on in the dark hallway.

"Ready?" Louis asked.

I led the way into the parking lot and then out onto
Atlantic Avenue. Even at four in the morning, the street

was packed—not stop-and-go, but almost as much traffic as you'd see during a normal weekday afternoon. Late-coming tourists—or "pilgrims," as Brita had started calling them— were trying their hardest to make it down here for the launch and the ultimate close encounter. Of course, if we did everything right, they'd be going home disappointed. Or maybe not. I really had no idea.

Louis took point, with Dru and me following.

After we rode awhile without incident, Louis stopped at a light and Dru and I pulled up next to him.

Dru looked back. "We're being followed."

"What?" Louis said. "By who?"

"A red SUV," Dru answered. "It's been tailing us for the last few blocks."

"It's Brita's," I told them.

Louis looked back. "I thought she was on the air. Up at the crack of dawn, special report covering the launch and all."

"Then it's Dr. Gleeman," Dru concluded.

"We've got to lose them! This way!" Louis led us to the right, off into the side streets. It'd take us a little longer to get to Louis's house, but assuming Dr. Gleeman didn't know where we were going, we could probably escape in the dark.

We pedaled furiously for a few minutes, taking random turns but trying to go generally toward Louis's house.

After a while, we paused at a stop sign.

"Did we lose them?" Louis asked.

"I think so," I said.

"But we picked up someone else," Dru stated. "Look!" She pointed behind us, where the streetlights hit a darkened sedan a couple blocks back.

"Let's go!" Louis shouted, and began pedaling. He crossed the intersection and then sped left, Dru and I racing behind.

As we took a turn and got to the next intersection, a

minivan pulled in front of us and screeched to a halt. Louis barely had time to stop before plowing into it.

I wasn't so lucky.

As I pulled myself off the ground, the door of the minivan opened and a familiar voice rang out. "Don't sit there! Get in before they see you!"

"Mrs. *Fleance?*" I exclaimed, still a little stunned from my crash. "What are you doing here?"

"I'll explain on the way!" she said. "Right now, you need a boat, and they know you're going to Louis's house, and they'll never let you through the Lock!"

"Wait, *what*?" Louis asked.

"Leave the bikes and get in!" Mrs. Fleance said. Then she focused on him. "I'm sorry, hon, but you're going to have to ditch the leg. They're listening in on the real-time telemetry to track you."

"What?" he exclaimed. "Who? Dr. Gleeman?"

"No, the government," Mrs. Fleance replied. She pointed behind us at a black car. "There they are! Hurry! Get in!"

"Do it!" Dru said as she clambered off her bike and dived into the van. A moment later, Louis and I joined her, and Mrs. Fleance sped off.

"Get rid of the leg!" Mrs. Fleance yelled as she took a right turn too fast.

Louis hesitated, his face pale. "This thing is really, really expensive," he whispered. "Like, more-expensive-than-my-house expensive."

"Can't we block the signal or disable the transmitter or something?" I put in.

"No," Mrs. Fleance said, "but I'll make sure you get a new one!"

"How?" Louis and I demanded at the same time.

"Because it's *my* company that makes them!" Mrs. Fleance replied with an exasperated snort. "Now, if you want to help the girl return to her people, toss it!"

"You *own* AesProCorp?" Louis said.

"My grandson does now, but my husband and I founded it," she replied. "So, yes, I still have influence—"

"The surfers!" I interjected. "They recognized you! That's why they dropped Ishmael! You scared them to death!"

Mrs. Fleance continued in a rush. "We're the Pro Tour sponsors. No surfer on the eastern seaboard is going to cross me. I'm among the wealthiest people in the hemisphere, and I can buy you fifty legs like that one from the cash in my cookie jar! Now get rid of it!"

With reluctance, Louis undid the Velcro and pulled the prosthetic off his thigh. Opening the side door, he held the leg out.

"Do it like you mean it!" Mrs. Fleance snapped.

"Oh, man," he said, closing his eyes and dropping the leg into the street. "Have I ever mentioned that I really hate your slogan?"

I reached around him and pulled the door shut as Mrs. Fleance took a left and doubled back the way we came.

For a moment, Louis just sat there.

"Thanks," I told him.

He grunted.

"Where are we going?" Dru asked from behind me.

"I have a slip up at the Port," Mrs. Fleance said, "on the Atlantic side of the Lock."

"How did you know about any of this?" Louis asked.

She grimaced. "Well, now."

I leaned forward.

"The thing is . . ." she said.

"Yes?" Louis asked.

"On the UFO Boards, I'm Kurt186 from Berlin."

"*What?*" Louis exclaimed.

"I'm Kurt186 from Berlin."

"That's impossible," Louis said. "You've been here in Cocoa Beach the whole time! How could you possibly know about what's going on at Baikonur?"

"Well, dear," Mrs. Fleance replied, "one of the nice things about having more money than some countries is that you can hire people to observe things for you."

"So, you've been . . . *spying* on me, too?" Louis looked stunned. And, honestly, it did sound freaky.

"Not exactly," Mrs. Fleance said as she took another tight corner too fast. "I have an interest in this type of thing, and on the UFO Boards, it's much easier being a nineteen-year-old German boy studying for his *Abitur* than a seventy-five-year-old Floridian multimillionaire grandmother of two."

"I don't think we're being followed anymore," Dru put in from the back.

"Good." Mrs. Fleance turned onto a main street and sped into the Port.

"I don't understand," Dru said. "Why don't you run the company anymore?"

"Committee meetings," Mrs. Fleance answered. "And lawyers. Too many of both." She shrugged. "I got tired of it all a few years back, and now I just do special projects."

"Like my leg," Louis said.

"Yes," she replied. "And the alien body in the back seat."

"What?" We all spun to look.

"It's Ishmael!" Dru exclaimed. "How?"

Mrs. Fleance looked at Dru and me through the rear-view mirror. "You didn't really expect me to buy that line about the pig, did you?"

"Did *you* make the anonymous call to Dr. Gleeman?" I asked. "About alien body parts at the motel?"

Mrs. Fleance took a left. "Yes, I wanted them to get discredited in hopes that they'd back off, not that it seems to have worked."

Dru piped up from the back. "Why are you helping us?"

We raced into the marina. "I want you to take me with you to outer space."

Dru gasped. "Why?"

Mrs. Fleance shrugged. "I've done many things in my life, and I don't have much longer in this world, so I thought I might as well try to see the next." She brought the van to a stop. "Here we are."

"*This* is your boat?" Louis exclaimed as he hopped out, leaning first on the side of the van for balance, then on me. Tied up at the dock was a sleek, candy-apple-red Cigarette racing boat.

"Forty-nine-foot Grand Sport," Mrs. Fleance said. "Twin

racing engines. The whole shebang. Just picked it up for a steal at government auction."

"Awesome," I said.

"Man," Louis said to Mrs. Fleance as he maneuvered into his seat. "I really hope you're not messing with me."

"I'll give you three." She started the engine, and I untied the boat.

"Legs, not boats," she added.

Moments later, we were all aboard, and Mrs. Fleance was taking us at a fast idle away from the slip and into the Port.

I sat in the cockpit on the left, across the aisle from Mrs. Fleance at the helm. Louis and Dru sat in the bucket seats behind us.

We moved off slowly, without lights, to avoid being seen.

"Uh-oh," Mrs. Fleance said as we headed past the cruise ship berths.

"What is it?" I asked.

"Coast Guard," Mrs. Fleance said, nodding to a red-and-white cutter coming up on our port side. "The feds are still after you."

# 22

"I WAS HOPING WE WOULDN'T HAVE TO DO THIS

"I was hoping we wouldn't have to do this right away," Mrs. Fleance said.

"Do what?" I asked.

"This," Mrs. Fleance said.

I was thrust back into my seat as the boat leaped forward, bow in the air. Over the roar of the engines, I yelled, "Are you sure this is a good idea?"

She gave me a dismissive wave, but eased off marginally on the throttle. By then, we were far ahead of the Coast Guard cutter and approaching the open Atlantic.

"How much longer until the launch?" Dru asked.

"T minus thirty-nine minutes and counting," Louis yelled after checking his phone. "Everything seems to be on schedule."

Dru unzipped her backpack and pulled out a black plastic

object about the size of a brick. Using two hands, she set it on the console between her and Louis's seats.

"That's your communicator?" I asked.

"Yeah, why?" she replied, one hand still holding on to it.

"I was just expecting . . . never mind," I said.

Dru flipped a switch on the box, and a blue light began to blink. "I've activated the signal to my people! They should be able to detect it now, even above the noise that Gleeman's putting up!"

The boat leaped forward again as we cleared the Port entrance. Behind us, the Coast Guard cutter was far enough away that we couldn't see it anymore.

I turned back to Mrs. Fleance. "Are we outside the no-boating area?"

"Yes," she said, pointing at her GPS monitor.

The picture was clear, free of snowy interference. Which meant her little silver coin was working. I grabbed the pair of binoculars hanging from the handle of the cabin door.

"Do you know where we're going?" Dru called from behind me. "We've got to get near the site of the crash!"

"We can't miss it!" Mrs. Fleance yelled. She pointed forward and slightly to the left. "That's the USS *San Jacinto*!"

The cruiser was lit up from bow to stern. We could

make out the conning tower and, through the binoculars, the gun turret and missile launchers on deck. The ship was moving slowly, escorting a salvage ship, whose derricks and cranes were also lit up in stark white light.

"Have they spotted us?" I asked.

"That's an Aegis-type guided missile cruiser!" Louis yelled. "Of course they've spotted us!"

It occurred to me that it wasn't a good idea to be approaching a US Navy ship at sixty miles an hour in the dead of night . . . without lights.

"Maybe we should slow down," Dru said.

"T minus thirty minutes and counting!" Louis yelled.

At that moment, there was a loud clunking noise. The boat shuddered from deep within the hull. I was thrown forward into the bulkhead, and Dru's transmitter skittered to the floor at my feet.

"What was that?" Louis asked, half out of his seat.

That's when I noticed we were moving a lot slower than we had been a moment before.

Mrs. Fleance banged the cockpit console. "We lost the starboard engine!"

While she was talking, I picked up Dru's transmitter and held it out to her. "Uh-oh." The box was broken in half along a seam. The blue light was off.

"The epoxy didn't hold," Dru murmured, testing the pieces. "Anyone have a rubber band?"

"Why would any of us have a—" Louis began, but I tapped him on the arm with the back of my hand. "Oh."

Solemnly, I handed over the silver-gray wristband Louis had given me a lifetime ago.

Dru slipped it over the box, securing its halves. After a brief adjustment, the blue light started blinking. Satisfied that it was working, she looked at me quizzically. "Why are you guys wearing matching rubber bands anyway?"

"It's to prevent you from picking up our mental auras," I told her.

"Oh, that wouldn't work at all," she replied as she set the communicator back on the armrest. "For that, you need aluminum foil."

I was almost positive she was joking. Then it occurred to me. "Mrs. Fleance," I said. "You're Kurt186. Where's *your* wristband?"

She chuckled. "You should know better than to ask a lady to tell her secrets."

Louis coughed. "Told you it would be useful." Then he glanced at his phone again. "T minus twenty-seven minutes and counting."

Dru pointed behind us. "They're gaining!"

The lights of the Coast Guard cutter shone more brightly as it closed the distance.

"I'm going as fast as we can," Mrs. Fleance said, casting a worried glance back.

"The *San Jacinto* is coming this way!" Louis said. The cruiser was moving slowly in our direction, trying to get between us and the salvage ship.

Dru glanced at the radio transmitter. "What about the launch?"

"It's on!" Louis said.

That's when the lights of the cruiser went dark. The salvage ship went black at the same time. Behind us, the Coast Guard cutter suffered the same fate.

So did the entire Space Coast. Exactly like the last time. But thanks to the silver disk, we were still moving as fast as we could with only one engine.

Mrs. Fleance flipped a switch and our running lights went on. Then she cut back on the throttle and held us steady. For a moment, there was near silence. The only sound was the idle thrum of the boat's engine as the craft gently bobbed on the waves.

"There's another boat!" Louis said, looking astern.

It wasn't the Coast Guard, though. It was a big Bay-liner with lights on, fast approaching.

I looked through the binoculars. "It's Dr. Gleeman and Brita!"

"I don't think they matter anymore," Mrs. Fleance replied, her voice soft.

Moments later, their boat pulled alongside ours, the camera pointing our way.

Ahead, off the starboard bow, a gigantic patch of water began to roil. The brownish-green ocean bubbled with foam and bright white lights.

"They're surfacing," Dru said. She was smiling.

As soon as she'd spoken, the spaceship emerged from the ocean. It rose to hover, water cascading down, about fifty feet in the air above us. It was that same triangular ship we'd seen the night of the first launch.

The Cigarette boat rocked in the waves the spacecraft was making. Water sloshed over the bow.

That's the last thing I noticed before the world went white. Then black.

# 23

THERE'S LIGHT AND I'M COLD. THERE'S WETNESS.

There are strange shapes and pentagons and big eyes.

I'm swimming and weightless. I have gray skin and I'm cold.

There's pain.

I see something that lives at the bottom of the Europan oceans that looks like a Christmas tree but is ambulatory and carnivorous.

I see and remember.

Everything.

. . . . . . . . . . . . . . . . . . . . . . . . . . . . . . . . . . . . . . . . . . . . . . . . . . . . . . . . .

There was a car. Erica was driving. Louis was seated next to her, and I was asleep in the back and it was dark out. The car was entering an intersection, and the light was green.

A truck was speeding toward the same crossing from the right. To the left, a bright light appeared in the sky: a blue-green sphere with rings around it. The streetlights and the stoplights went off, and the truck on the right didn't stop.

Louis screamed.

Then I saw a room, brightly lit, but I couldn't make out a source for the light.

And then I was at the motel and I was also in a strange fluid environment where I somehow felt like I belonged . . .

# 24

THE FIRST THING I SAW WHEN I WOKE UP WAS A

tall alien standing next to my bed looking down at me. He reached over to help me sit up.

We were in a dark room, with only my bed and a bed across a narrow aisle from me lit up with white lights. Sitting on that other bed was me. Alien-me in alien form, not human-me. He lifted a hand and smiled.

"Thank you," I said, grinning. I lifted my own hands and stared at them. I wiggled my fingers like I hadn't done it in years. Which, technically, I guess, I hadn't.

A moment later, another small gray approached to stand at the foot of both beds.

It was Dru. "I'm glad you're better. We're going to send you home now."

"Wait," I told her. I hesitated. I wasn't sure what to say, but I knew we owed her a lot.

"I'll be coming, too," she replied.

"Wait. What?" I asked.

She cocked her head. "Tad and I have things we want to do."

"Tad . . ." I began, and then it hit me as the alien in the other bed got up and walked over to stand beside her. "You're her brother! The one flying the ship the night of the accident!"

He nodded. "I was the only one close enough to make the Change."

"I know," I said, to my surprise. And I did. I remembered everything he remembered. It felt really, really strange. I look over at Dru. "You're really coming with us?"

"For a while." She shrugged. "In any case, I have to get my cleaning deposit back."

# 25

THE NEXT THING I WAS REALLY CONSCIOUS OF was the sun shining high overhead and a group of us standing on an open, pitching deck. Next to me, Louis stumbled on an unfamiliar pair of crutches, but was able to stay upright.

It took me a second, but then I realized we were on the helicopter pad at the stern of the *San Jacinto*, the guided-missile cruiser that had been escorting the salvage ship. It took me a moment longer to recognize everyone who was there.

Louis. Dru. Dr. Gleeman. Mrs. Fleance. Brita Carnegie. The camera guy.

There was also a blond woman I didn't know.

"Kate Johnson!" Brita exclaimed, snapping her fingers and staring at the stranger.

"It is!" Mrs. Fleance said.

I suddenly understood. "Is she one of the missing blondes?"

As Brita and Mrs. Fleance crowded around Kate, who apparently *had* been one of the missing blondes, I looked at Louis.

"Are you human-Aidan or alien-Aidan?" he asked, stumbling a little as the ship lurched in a swell.

"Human-Aidan," I told him. I held out my hands, turning them over, flexing my fingers. I grinned and then, just to mess with him, said, "I think." I gestured with a hand. "You've still got the thermal imager."

It was hooked onto his belt loop. He grabbed the camera and pointed it at me.

Before he could tell me what he saw, we were surrounded by the ship's crew, several of whom were armed with M16s. The United States Navy, we discovered, tends to frown on people who mysteriously appear on their ships.

We were hustled into a conference room while Mrs. Fleance demanded to know what had happened to her boat.

We found out that the Cigarette boat and the Bayliner were tied up alongside, although they'd been swamped when the alien spaceship had surfaced. That was probably why Dru's people had taken everyone aboard.

Long and short of it, we'd been gone a day and a half, the launch had been canceled (again), there had been another blackout when we'd returned, and there were still a gazillion people on the beach.

# 26

THE NAVY KEPT US SEPARATED ABOARD SHIP for a few days as guests "for observation," during which time we all had several long conversations with men in black suits.

Brita, Dr. Gleeman, and Kate Johnson, it seemed, remembered nothing.

The rest of us weren't talking.

. . . . . . . . . . . . . . . . . . . . . . . . . . . . . . . . . . . . . . . . . . . . . . . . . . . . . . . . . . . . . . . . . . . . . . .

Four days into our stay aboard the *San Jacinto*, the launch finally went off.

By this time, the government apparently decided we weren't a threat or contagious or anything. The captain let us all onto the command deck for the occasion, and we had a view from the wing of the bridge as the rockets' glare lit the night sky.

Once the clipper was safely in orbit, everyone else went back inside to have a drink in the captain's cabin. Finally, for the first time since we'd returned, there was just Dru, Louis, and me.

"I met me," I told Louis. "Alien-me."

He pivoted on his good leg to face me. I couldn't read his expression. "I know. I saw." He paused. "Two years as an alien, though. I would've sworn you were a freak a lot longer."

We laughed, even though it wasn't that funny.

"So Tad and Mrs. Fleance Changed?" I asked Dru. "You said you had things to do."

Dru grinned, but wouldn't say any more.

Louis unhooked the FLIR camera from his belt. "I could use this."

"But you won't," Dru replied.

He nodded.

For a long time, we all were silent.

"What now?" Louis asked finally, as the launch contrail dissipated in the wind.

"Back to the motel," I told him.

Home.

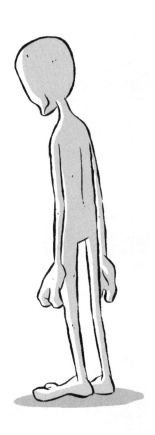

# AUTHOR'S NOTE

around Cocoa Beach and the Cape Canaveral area, certain geographic liberties have been taken.

The Mercury Inn and Suites is fictional, though it is inspired by a certain motel in Cocoa Beach that my family stayed at many times on vacation when I was growing up.

The space clipper *Resolution* is likewise fictional, an imagined successor to the space shuttle. The *Resolution*'s countdown sequence is based generally on the one used during the space shuttle program.

AesProCorp and the AP Sporting Goods and Surf Shop Extraordinaire are fictional.

# ACKNOWLEDGMENTS

THEY SAY "WRITE WHAT YOU KNOW." SADLY, I have never had a close encounter with aliens from outer space.

However, when I was a kid, my parents would take my brother and me on vacation to Florida. We lived in Chicago, and this usually meant driving down in the station wagon and staying at various motels and seeing sights along the way. I'd like to say thanks to them for such memories, which provided an inspiration for *Little Green Men at the Mercury Inn*.

I'd also like to thank the late Bernie and Stefan Gwiazda, my parents' best friends, who moved from Chicago when I was a kid to buy that certain motel in Cocoa Beach that we visited so often, and who were like an additional pair of favorite aunts and uncles.

Thanks also to Alison Dellenbaugh and K. A. Holt for reading an early draft; and to Carol Lynch Williams and the 2010 Austin SCBWI Master Class for input on (an even earlier) first five pages.

Finally, thanks to my wife, Cynthia Leitich Smith, who read countless drafts and has been so supportive of the writing habit.